Bullfighting

Roddy Doyle

VINTAGE CANADA

Published in Canada by Vintage Canada, a division of Random House of Canada Limited, Toronto, in 2011, and simultaneously in hardcover in the United Kingdom by Jonathan Cape, a division of The Random House Group UK, London. Distributed by Random House of Canada Limited.

Vintage Canada with colophon is a registered trademark.

www.randomhouse.ca

Library and Archives Canada Cataloguing in Publication

Doyle, Roddy, 1958–
Bullfighting / Roddy Doyle.

Issued also in electronic format.

ISBN 978-0-307-40113-7

I. Title.

PR6054.O95B85 2011   823'.914   C2010-906690-1

Typeset in StempelGaramond by Palimpsest Book Production Limited, Falkirk, Stirlingshire.

Printed and bound in the United States of America

2 4 6 8 9 7 5 3 1

Dedicated to Ronnie Caraher, Paul Corcoran
and John Sutton

The stories in this work originally appeared in the following: 'Recuperation', 'The Photograph', 'Teaching', 'The Joke', 'Ash', 'The Dog', 'Bullfighting', 'Sleep', in the *New Yorker*; 'The Slave', a longer version, in *Speaking with the Angel*, ed. Nick Hornby; 'Blood', in *Stories: All New Tales*, ed. Neil Gaiman and Al Sarrantonio; 'The Plate', in the *Guardian*; 'Animals', in *The News from Dublin*, ed. Joseph O'Connor. 'Recuperation' also appeared in *New Dubliners*, ed. Oona Frawley, and 'The Joke' also appeared in *The Faber Book of New Irish Short Stories: 2004–05*, ed. David Marcus.

Contents

Recuperation

He walks. Every day, he walks. That was what the doctor had said. All the doctors. Plenty of exercise, they'd told him. It was the one thing he'd really understood.

—Are you a golf man, Mr Hanahoe?

—No.

—Hill walking?

—No.

—Do you walk the dog?

—No dog.

He'd buried the dog a few years ago, in the back garden.

—We'll have to get you exercising.

—Okay.

He walks now, every day. Sundays too. He hadn't even liked the dog. He walks, the same way. Except maybe when it was a pup, and the kids were younger. Every day, the same way. The way he went the first day. Up the Malahide Road.

Hanahoe walks.

When the dog died the kids were upset, but not upset enough to go out in the rain and dig the grave. The dog had been dying for years; the kids were living most of their time outside the house. It had been up to Hanahoe.

He starts at the Artane roundabout, his back to town, facing Malahide.

He starts.

He'd have waited till it stopped raining, but it didn't seem right, and it had been raining for days. So he dug in the dark. It was easy work, the ground was so wet. The spade sank nicely for him. And he dug up a rabbit. He saw it in the torchlight. A skeleton. He'd buried the rabbit years before: before the dog, after the goldfish.

It takes him ten minutes to get to the Artane roundabout but he doesn't count that. The walk starts, the exercise starts, when he's on the corner of Ardlea Road and the Malahide Road.

He had meant to tell the kids about the rabbit. He threw it back in, on top of the dog. He'd meant to tell them about it the next morning, before work and school. It was the only time they were all together in the house. But, he remembers now as he walks, he never did tell them. And he didn't throw the rabbit in. He lowered it, on the spade, and let it slide off, onto the dog. He forgot to tell them. He thinks he forgot. He's not sure.

There are other places he could walk. There are plenty of places. He could get in the car and drive to St Anne's or Bull Island, or the path along the coast, or even out to Howth. But he doesn't. He's not sure why, just certain that he won't. But that's not true. He does know why; he knows exactly why. It's people. Too many people.

He got out of the habit of talking. As the kids were getting older. He put a stone slab, left over from the patio, over the dog's grave, and then remembered that there was no dog now to dig it up. There was no need for the slab. Another thing he was going to tell the kids, and didn't.

This is the stretch that Hanahoe has chosen. Starting outside the old folks' flats. Mount Dillon Court. He's never seen anyone coming out of there. Old or young – a milkman or Garda, a daughter, grandchild. No one. And that suits him. He'd stop looking if he saw anyone.

—Do you get down to the pub at all?

—No.

—The golf club?

—You asked me that the last time. No.

He used to. He went to the pub now and again. Once a week, twice. Sometimes after mass. She came too. He thought she'd liked it. He'd always thought that. A pint for him, something different for her. Gin and tonic, vodka and something, Ballygowan, Baileys. She'd never settled on one drink. And he doesn't remember ever thinking there was anything wrong with that.

He walks past the old cottages. They're out of place there, on the dual carriageway. He walks beside the cycle path. To the newer houses. They're on a road that runs beside the main road. They're well back and hidden, behind old hedges and trees. If people look out at him passing every day, he doesn't care, and he doesn't have to. He doesn't know them, and he won't. He walks on the grass. The ground is hard. It hasn't rained in a long time.

He wears tracksuit bottoms. She bought them for him. They were in a bag at the end of the bed when he got home from the hospital. Champion Sports. Two tracksuits. A blue and a grey. He doesn't wear the tops. And he won't. He doesn't know when she moved into their daughters' bedroom; he's not sure, exactly. It was empty for a while. After the eldest girl moved out, and then her sister. And then she'd moved in, after a few months. He has trainers as well, that he got himself after he came home. The first time he went out, up to Artane Castle. There was no row or anything when she moved into the girls' room. He doesn't think there was. He woke up one night, and she wasn't there. And the next night he felt her getting out of bed. It was too hot, she said. The night after that, she said nothing. The night after, she went straight to the girls' room. A few years ago. Two, three. The trainers still look new. She never came back to their room. And he never asked why not. He's been wearing them for a month now. They still look new-white. It annoys him.

Past Chanel Road. Past the Rampaí sign. He's at the turn-off for Coolock. He looks behind, checks for cars. He's clear, he crosses. Chanel to the left, the school. The kick-boxing sign on the gate pillar. Juniors and Seniors, Mondays and Fridays. They'd nothing like that when his kids were younger. Kick-boxing. Martial arts. Skateboarding. Nothing like that – he thinks.

4

Hanahoe crosses the road.

—Are you a joiner?

—What?

—Do you join? Clubs. Societies.

—No.

—No, yet, or no, never?

He doesn't answer. He shrugs.

He used to be. He thought he was. A joiner. The residents, the football. Fundraising, bringing kids to the matches. He did it. He did them all. He'd enjoyed it. Then his sons stopped playing, and he stopped going. Less people to talk to – it just happened that way. He didn't miss it at the time. He doesn't miss it now.

He passes the granite stone, 'Coolock Village' carved into it, 'Sponsored by Irish Shell Ltd, 1998'. He's behind the petrol station, the second-hand cars, against the back wall. Behind the chipper, and Coolock Glass. A high wall, there's nothing to see. To his right, the traffic. Too early for the rush, but it's heavy enough. He wonders what kick-boxing is like, what kick-boxing parents are like. He hasn't a clue. He's at the church now, the car park. There's nothing on – funeral, wedding – no one there. He enjoyed the football. He liked the men who ran the club – he remembers that, he remembers saying it. There was a trip to Liverpool – the car, the ferry. Three kids in the back, another father beside him. That had been good. A good weekend. Liverpool had won. Against Ipswich or Sunderland. Some team like that.

He's doing well. He's not tired. It's hot. It might rain. Another high wall, the backs of more houses. He has to bend under branches. Southampton. A bus passes, knocks warm air against him. Liverpool beat Southampton. The bus swerves in, to the stop in front of him. A woman gets off. She walks away. She's faster than him; he won't see her face. She wears trainers, like his.

He stopped going to mass. She still goes. As far as he knows. He stopped going when the kids stopped. He's coming up to the crossroads. There's one of the Africans there, selling the *Herald*. Walking between the cars at the lights. He's never seen anyone buy one. But the Africans are there, every day.

He can cross; the light is green for him. Cadbury's, down to the left. More houses, in off the road. He hated mass, the whole thing. Always did. Standing up, sitting down. Most Sundays. Or Saturday nights, when they started that. Getting it over with.

He's at the back of Cadbury's now. It's like a park. Greenhouses and all. It's like the countryside here, the little river, the trees. What it must have been like. But not in his memory. It was always like this.

It's depressing, a life, laid out like that. Mass, driving the kids to football, or dancing. The pint on Friday. The sex on Sunday. Pay on Thursday. The shop on Saturday. Leave the house at the same time, park in the same spot. The loyalty card. The bags. The routine. One day he knew: he hated it.

His mother worked in Cadbury's when he was a kid. Christmas and Easter. The cinema across the road. The UCI. He hasn't been to the pictures in years. She used to bring home Easter eggs, the ones that were out of shape, no use for the shops. He brought one into school. His lunch. King of the world that day. He can't remember the last film he went to. He's starting to sweat. Fine. That's exercise. That's what they want. He can smell the Tayto factory. It's not too bad today. Clouds gathering, ahead. Getting ready. It's hot. *Michael Collins*. The last film he went to. But that's a long time ago. He's sure he's been since then. He looks across at the UCI. But he can't read the names of the films. Too far away. He hasn't a clue what's on, what's big. No kids at home now. He's going past the paint factory. He thinks it's a paint factory. AkzoNobel. Berger, Sandtex, Sadolin. She doesn't go to the pictures either. He doesn't think she does. She didn't like *Michael Collins*. He did.

More country cottages. And more behind them, old lanes, warehouses. He's coming up to Woodie's. She meets her friends when she goes out – he thinks. She still tells him, sometimes. Before she goes. Tells him she's going. Who she's meeting. A gang of women she's known for years. He knows them all. He knows their husbands. They used to go out together, the men and the women. It wasn't too bad. Not now though, not in years. Maybe she goes to the pictures with them. He doubts it. She'd tell him. It's not that they never talk. She went to a play, a few months back. In town. She told him. Something like that, she'd tell him. He'd tell her. It's not that bad.

He hates Woodie's. Not the shop. He sees the need – wood, paint. He opens his jacket. It's a bit too hot now. He's fine. He's grand. The heart is calm. It's not the products. It's the idea. The DIY. The people who live in the place at the weekend. Haunting the aisles. And the other shops over there. Classic Furniture. Right Price Tiles. 'Tile Your Bathroom For €299.' The pet shop's gone. The big place. He used to go there with the kids. She'd come with them. They laughed when they realised: it was a family outing. Nearer than the zoo. Ice cream on the way home. The kids were delighted. The innocence. It was lovely.

He looks behind. Before he crosses. It's usually busy. Nothing coming; he doesn't have to stop. The McDonald's is new. Toymaster. PC Superstore. And Lidl. Only open a week. Some kind of supermarket. The car park is fuller, packed since it opened.

He doesn't know when it changed. He doesn't know when he knew. Before she moved out of the bedroom. They stopped talking. There was nothing dramatic.

He's been living alone for years. He doesn't know what happened. There was no shouting, very little. There was no violence. No one was hit. No one played away from home. He didn't. She didn't.

There was a Christmas do. He's coming up to the Texaco station. The pub is behind it. Newtown House. Two doors, no windows. The Belcamp Inn, it used to be called – he thinks. The only place, the only time he was ever in a fight. In the days when he took his time coming home. He looks behind, crosses the turn for the industrial estate. Friday night. He knocked into a guy at the bar. Not really a fight. Just a couple of digs – he was too scared to feel them. Then too scared to leave.

That Christmas do. A young one who'd just started in

the job a few weeks before. His leg had touched hers, sitting together. He was surprised when she didn't move. A bit scared. Her leg pressed against his. Nothing sexy about it. Nice, though. The thought. Then they'd met in the corridor. Him going to the toilet, her coming back. They smiled. He stopped. She didn't. Then she did. He put his hands on her. They kissed. Rubbed each other. He was bursting, full of drink. They stopped. He went to the jacks, came back, and it never happened. That was it.

That was all. He never told anyone.

He looks. Cars coming up behind him. He waits, and crosses the station entrance. It's not as fancy as those new forecourts going up everywhere. Martina. Good-looking girl. She was young. But so was he.

That was all.

He doesn't know what happened. Or what he'd say, how he'd bring it up, after this long.

—What went wrong?

He could never say that.

—What happened?

She'd look at him. He'd have to explain. Where would he start? He hadn't a clue. And the question would announce it – the end. They'd have to admit it. And one of them would have to go.

Him.

But he's alone already. He knows the last time he spoke to someone. This morning. Getting the paper. The woman behind the counter.

—Nice day again.

—Yeah.

That was it. A nice woman. Attractive. His age. A bit younger. He's coming up to the Darndale roundabout. He never looked at women his age. Until recently. They were always too old. Not really women; ex-women. Now, though, he looks. But he doesn't. Not really. He doesn't know what he'd do if a woman spoke to him.

—Nice day again.

—Yeah.

What else could he say? He isn't interested. He's used to himself. He's fine. He's come to the roundabout. He'll go on. He isn't tired. He crosses. Darndale to the left. Rough spot. He's never been in there. He runs the last bit, trots – to the other side. He's fine.

It's dark, very quickly. Like four hours gone, in a second. And cold, and it's raining. He goes on. He closes his jacket. It's bucketing. There's an inch of sudden water. He can't see far. The traffic noise has changed; it's softer, menacing.

Who's to blame? No one. It just happened. It's too late now. He can't pull them back, his wife, the kids. They have their own lives. She does; they do. Maybe grandkids will do something. If there are any. He doesn't know. He knows nothing. He feels nothing. He doesn't even feel sorry for himself. He doesn't think he does.

He's fine. He copes.

But this is stupid. It's lashing, no sign of sunlight. He's cold. His feet are wringing. He turns back. He can feel the water down his back. It annoys him, giving up, but he's – not sure – reassured, or something. He can change his mind. He's prepared to.

He makes it to the bus shelter. Across the Malahide Road. A break in the traffic. He goes through the water. He's fine. In under the shelter. A gang of young guys. Fuckin' this, fuckin' that. Rough kids. Too skinny, too fat. Not really kids. One of them pushes him. Bangs against him. An accident. No apology. They laugh. They shove each other, out from the shelter.

He'll go. But one of them steps out, shouts. A taxi stops. They pile in. One slips. They laugh. They're gone.

There's one kid left there. A girl. Eight, nine – he's not sure. White tracksuit. Mousy hair, beads in it. She's chewing gum. His own kids were scared of gum, when they were little. His fault – he was always afraid of them choking. She's chewing away. He can hear her.

The rain is dying.

She speaks.

—I'm waitin' on me mammy.

He's surprised. He says nothing, at first.

—Where is she?

—At her work, she says.—Comin' home.

—On the bus?

—Yeah.

—That's nice.

—Yeah.

He puts his hand out.

—The rain's stopping.

—It was badly needed, she says.

He smiles.

—You're dead right, he says.

11

The ground is already steaming. He shakes water from his jacket.

—I'll go on, he says.—Will you be alright there by yourself?

—Ah yeah, she says.—I'm grand.

—Good, he says.—Well. Seeyeh.

—Seeyeh.

The rain is gone. It's bright again.

He walks.

Nice kid. He smiles.

Hanahoe walks home.

The Photograph

Getting older wasn't too bad. The baldness suited Martin. Everyone said it. He'd had to change his trouser size from 34 to 36. It had been a bit of a shock, but it was kind of nice wearing loose trousers again, hitching them up when he stood up to go to the jacks, or whatever. He was fooling himself; he knew that. But that was the point – he *was* fooling himself. He'd put on weight but he felt a bit thinner.

There were other things too, that had nothing to do with his body and ageing. The kids getting older was one, and the freedom he'd kind of forgotten about. For years, if he stayed in bed in the morning, if he wanted to, it had to be carefully planned. Lizzie, his wife, had to be told. The kids had to be told, and nearly asked. It hadn't been worth it, the fuckin' palaver he'd had to go through. For years, all those years the kids were growing up, he'd been on call. A pal of his had used the phrase, *on call*. He'd been talking about his own life, but – there were four of them there that night in the local, sitting around one of the high tables – he'd been describing all their lives.

—I'm like a doctor without the fuckin' money, Noel had said.

They'd all smiled and nodded.

He'd loved it, mostly, the whole family/kids things, and he'd ignored the throb above his left eye that had often felt like too much coffee or dehydration, too much or too little of something, that he thought now had probably been the pressure of that life. For years, the throb – the vein. Everything he'd done, everywhere he'd gone. Every minute had been counted and used. He had four children, and there were eleven years between the oldest and the youngest. It was over now – it seemed to be over – and the throb had gone away.

It had taken a while. He'd be wide awake early on Saturday, with nothing to do. He'd drive down to the recycling centre in Coolock with five empty bottles and a cardboard box. He'd shove the box in on top of the other boxes and newspapers and he'd remember holding up one of the kids, usually the little girl, so she could reach the slot the cardboard was pushed into. He'd wonder what the fuck he was doing up and out of the house when he could have been at home in bed. He'd drive out to Howth and watch other people buying fish. He'd feel useful while he was driving. There were no kids in the back, only more cars behind him in the rear-view mirror. It took him a good while to stop. Well over a year. He was driving long after the kids stopped needing him. But he did stop. He could relax now without thinking too much about it.

He wasn't on call any more, and Noel was dead.

He missed the kids. Two of them still lived at home. They smiled when they saw him. They sometimes stayed at the table for a few minutes after they'd finished eating, and they'd chat. They'd talk more to Lizzie than to him, but it was easy enough; it was nice. They'd been wise that way, him and Lizzie. They'd got through the teen years without too much grief. There'd been no drug habits or pregnancies, not too much puking and far less screaming than they'd heard coming from some of the other houses on the road. They were great kids. He missed them. If he thought of it, the fact that he didn't have children any more – if he'd been an actor, it was what he'd have done to make himself cry.

There was sex as well. That was a nice surprise. There'd always been sex, more or less, in among the nappies and the Calpol and school books. They'd never really stopped fancying each other. But the big surprise was some of the stuff they'd got up to since the kids had stopped being kids. Without any announcement or decision. She bit one of his nipples one night, and she'd never done that before. It hurt but, fuck, it woke him up. And he'd made her come – this was a different night – just by talking to her. So she'd said, anyway. She was hanging onto him and crying before he really knew what was going on. He just thought it was a bit of gas, whispering into her ear. He even put on an American accent, all that *pussy* and *cock* palaver. He was still just getting the hang of it, deciding what part of the States he was from, when she came. He'd never fuckin' forget it.

And there were other women. Women liked mature men. He'd read that somewhere, in a waiting room somewhere – the dentist or the doctor. Or it was just one of the things you grew up with. Women went for older men. He'd never believed it. Even when he changed it a bit, to *some* women, and *some* older men. He'd always thought it was a load of bollix. He still thought that, even more since he'd started noticing women looking at him, kind of giving him the eye. Not young ones – he didn't think he could have coped with that, smiling back at some gorgeous monster less than half his age. No, it was mature women, older women – *some* older women. One or two of them. There was a woman from up the road who always waved at him – she lived on the other side, nearer the shops – and she looked great from that distance. He'd looked up from the pile of newspapers in the Spar one Sunday morning, and she'd been right beside him. He smelt her perfume, and she looked nice up close too. She was dressed up a bit, in the old-fashioned Sunday way. And she blushed when she saw him –

—Hi.

—Hi.

She looked a bit flustered.

—Great day.

—Lovely.

He loved that, thinking that, that he'd knocked her off-course a bit, just by being there, older man himself,

16

in the Spar on a Sunday morning. He felt the heat in his own face. He bought his *Indo* and kind of drifted out of the shop, took his time. He hoped, half hoped, they'd walk back up the road together, and chat till they got to her place, and a little bit more at the gate, then he'd go on to his. But it didn't happen. He walked home alone, and she passed him in her car and she kept going, past her house. She must have been going somewhere, her ma's or somewhere. Her husband was driving.

It was fine. He wasn't interested in taking it further, and he didn't think he'd have had the guts. Anyway, another of his friends, Davie, had separated from his missis a few years back and he was living back home with his mother, the poor fucker, because he couldn't afford to do anything else. But he, Davie, went to a different pub on Sunday nights, where men and women like himself, unattached and out of practice, went. And, after a few months of this, he'd come up with Davie's Law: All women over the age of forty are mad. He'd announced it in the local, one of their Wednesday nights, and none of them had disagreed.

Martin was lucky, though. Lizzie was kind of sexy mad. The insanity suited her. She knew it, and that made it even better. He'd never have done anything to wreck it.

But it wasn't all great, the getting older business – far from. He'd started grunting whenever he picked something up or bent down to tie his laces, or whatever. He hated it. He'd tell himself to stop. But he'd forget. It became natural. Pick the soap up in the shower – grunt.

Start the lawnmower – grunt. He didn't have to grunt. He was well able to bend over and the rest of it. He asked the lads, and they all did it too.

And there was the cancer. Not his. He'd never had it. His friend who'd died. Noel. That was cancer. Felt a bit short of breath. Went to the doctor. Straight up to Beaumont Hospital. Came out two days later with the news and the dates for his chemotherapy. He told them about it the day after that, in the local, sitting in all the smoke – this was a few months before the smoking ban.

Martin didn't smoke. He never had. Noel did. But he'd given them up a year or so before the cancer, or at least before he found out about it.

None of them said anything, for a bit. They waited for him to go on, to make it less terrible. Martin watched Davie put out his cigarette, crush it into the ashtray. He pushed away the last of the rising smoke with his hand.

—They say it's early enough, Noel said.—With the chemo and that. They should be able to stop it.

And they'd watched him slowly die. Not slowly. Only now, it seemed slow, start to end. But at the time, he'd been fine – he'd looked fine. He'd lost the hair with the chemo, but he'd looked good. Into the second year, they'd all thought he was going to make it. But then it had really started. They'd had to visit his house. He sat there with his oxygen beside him, one of those canister things. His eyes started to look huge and he struggled to get up when he was going to the door to say goodbye to them.

—Stay where you are; we're grand.

—No, no, I'll come out with yis.

It took him forever to get to the door. They waved at the gate, and smiled back in at him and his mad skeleton smile, his shirt way too big on him.

They got into the car. And then they spoke.

—He's not going to make it, is he?

—No.

Then nothing for a while.

—We'd better get going. He'll be wondering why we're not moving.

—Right; okay.

Lizzie knew Noel wasn't well and she asked Martin how he was, every couple of days. She asked this time and he told her and he cried and she held his head. About a week after that, he went to the jacks and there was blood on the sides of the bowl when he stood up and turned to flush it. He'd pulled the handle before he properly knew: that was his blood. He said nothing. There was no blood the next time, or the time after that. But it was back the next time; it looked strange on the toilet paper, too red. He had to phone in sick and stay home, because he was getting cramps and sweating like a madman. He told Lizzie. He went back to bed. She sat beside him.

—Blood?

—Yeah, he said.

—Jesus. Sore?

—Kind of, he said. —Uncomfortable.

—I'll phone the doctor's, she said.

She looked at her watch.

—He should be still there.

—No, he said.

—Yes.

—Okay, he said.

He had to get up again. He had to go back to the jacks.

—You poor thing, she said.

He went past her.

—Sorry, he said.

He heard her at the toilet door, waiting. He wished she'd go away.

It wasn't cancer. He'd ended up going to a specialist and he had a colonoscopy three weeks later, a fibre-optic camera all the way to his appendix. He lay down on the bed-thing, turned on his left side, like he was told, and the specialist gave him the jab, a needle in the arm. It was over when he woke up and he was in a different room. They gave him toast and tea and the specialist was suddenly there, beside him – Martin was still a bit dopey – and told him that he had diverticular disease. The specialist wrote it down on a piece of paper, said something about looking it up on the Net, and then he went back behind the screen and Martin didn't see him again.

He googled it when he got home, and for a few stupid minutes, he wished he had cancer. It was fuckin' disgusting. *Diverticula are pockets that develop in the colon wall.* He could feel his own colon; he could feel it throbbing, coiling. He got up, and sat down again.

Pain, chills, fever, change in bowel habits. His finger was on the screen, under each word. *Perforation, abscess or fistula formation.* He found a dictionary in his daughter's room and looked up *abscess.* He'd never been sure what an abscess actually was, some kind of spectacular toothache. *A swollen area within body tissue, containing an accumulation of pus.* He put the dictionary back on her desk. He sat on her bed and ate the Mars bar he'd found beside the dictionary. He didn't look up *fistula.* It could wait. He knew enough.

He couldn't tell anyone. He couldn't tell Lizzie. She'd never let him touch her again. Or she would and he'd see it, the pity and revulsion.

Pus.

Stand well back, lads, the next time I fart. He could make a joke of it. He was good at that. It was part of the way they were, making a laugh out of everything. But they'd still all be disgusted.

Why him – why Martin? What had he done to deserve perforations and pus? Cancer was dignified, something nearly to be proud of – a fuckin' achievement, compared to this. What the fuck was a fistula formation? He still didn't look it up.

Noel was in the hospice. He was too weak for home. They went in to see him one Sunday afternoon, one of the last summer days. It was a nice room. The window was open. Martin could smell flowers, hear birds. Noel sat on the side of his bed. His head was bent and everything he said came through the oxygen mask. He sounded high-pitched, like his voice had never broken,

21

like every bit of each word was being pulled out of him. They chatted about the usual, the football and that. They laughed more than they had to, and then the laughter became more even and Martin thought he'd tell them about the diverticular thing. But Noel got in there first.

—Look it, he said.

They said nothing. They waited.

—I'm fighting this, he said.

They waited.

—Yis know that, he said.—But, in case.

They watched him swallow air and keep it.

—Yis've been. Great friends, he said.—I just wanted. To say that. In case. You know.

—Works both ways, brother, said Davie.

—You'll be grand, Noel.

—Just, wanted. To say it.

He died four days after.

The trick was the diet. As far as he could see, from what he'd read on Google. It wasn't really a disease. It was more like, waiting to be a disease. Most people who had it didn't even know. Plenty of fresh stuff, vegetables and that. No nuts or big seeds, nothing that might block one of the pockets on his colon.

For fuck sake.

My arse is a time bomb, lads. He could hear himself saying it. Making small of it. Maybe when they were having a pint after the funeral. He could see it and hear it. The questions, the laughter.

He told Lizzie.

He actually blamed Lizzie, but only for a little while. It was the food she'd been giving him for the last twenty-nine years. She'd been killing him. But he didn't really think that. He told her the same day Noel died. He should have waited – he thought that later. He shouldn't have jumped in with his own bad news. He knew he was doing it. Throwing himself into poor Noel's grave. But he did it.

—I've a thing called diverticular disease.

He stopped himself from adding *myself*. I've a thing called diverticular disease myself. He didn't go that far – I've got cancer too. He didn't. But it sat there. He knew it. On the kitchen table.

Disease.

He told her what it was, as far as he understood it.

—I can swing between constipation and diarrhoea. Or, if one of the yokes gets blocked.

He was stuck now. He had to go on. She was looking straight at him.

—If the faecal matter gets caught in one of them, he said.—One of the pockets or pouches, like. It'll become inflamed. Even perforated.

Her hand went to her mouth.

—If I'm not careful, he told her,—they'll have to take out my colon.

—All of it?

—Most of it.

He wasn't sure. He hadn't really read that far.

—But that's only if I'm not careful.

—What d'you mean, careful? she said.

—About my diet and that, he said.

—What's wrong with it?

—Nothing.

He was leaning over, taking the big words back off the table. Why hadn't he kept his fuckin' mouth shut?

—Will you have to become a vegetarian or something? she said.

—No, he said. —I don't think so. But I'll have to eat vegetables.

—You do already.

—I know.

Just don't boil them to fuck.

He didn't say it. He didn't even think it, really.

He shrugged.

—It's just . . . Anyway. Now you know.

They sat at the table. He thought about Noel.

They walked up to the church together, him and Lizzie; it was no distance from the house. There was a big crowd, waiting on the steps and on the bits of grass, out onto the street.

—That's good, he said to Lizzie.

He wasn't sure why. A bit of a comfort for Noel's wife and kids who'd be arriving soon in the black cars, with the hearse. It was what he'd have thought. My husband was popular. All these people knew my father. Familiar faces. Unfamiliar faces. He'd had a big, full life.

Martin had bought a new shirt, to go with his jacket. It was a bit tight on him, but grand as long as he kept the jacket on. He'd be losing weight soon. The whole new regime. Fruit, grains. The fresh veg. Legumes. Another of the words he'd had to find in the dictionary. Peas, beans. Health and boredom.

He hadn't slept. Not since Noel had died. Since a good bit before, actually. He'd jump awake before he was really asleep. Afraid to sleep. Afraid of falling. His skin was dry. He saw that when he brought his face up to the mirror. Dry skin all over his face. Especially across his forehead and at the sides of his nose. And spots. He could feel them, threatening, angry, right over his forehead. He looked desperate.

—Stress, said Lizzie.

He nodded.

—Grief.

—He's only dead a few days, he said.

—You've known for two years, she said back.

She was right. It made sense. The death, the news, hadn't done anything. He'd known what it was when the phone rang. He'd been waiting.

The sleep was the worst part. One good night would have made the difference, would have put whatever was missing back under his skin. That was how he felt, what he nearly believed. The night before, Lizzie had handed him a bottle of Benylin, the cough mixture, half empty and sticky. He hadn't seen Benylin since the kids had grown up.

—Take a mouthful of that.

He looked at it.

—What's the best-before date? he said.—It must be fuckin' ancient.

—Never mind the date, she said.—If it pours out it's grand.

He got the lid off. He filled his mouth. He'd always liked the taste of it. He swallowed.

—Here, she said.

He gave her the bottle. She put it to her mouth and swallowed the rest.

—Goodnight, she said.

—Goodnight.

He conked out but he was awake again at half-three. Wide awake. Looking at the ceiling becoming brighter, the big swinging cobweb he always meant to get at with the brush. He got up. Had his breakfast. His new breakfast – a sliced banana, a sliced pear. Yum fucking' yum. It was alright though, and good for him. He was hungry again by the time the rest of them got up.

They stood at the church gate and chatted a bit as they waited for the hearse. It was weird, like pretending they weren't there for the funeral.

—Here they come.

The hearse came off the road, and up, past them, to the front of the church. They blessed themselves. The coffin in there – Noel. It didn't seem real. And the black cars, after the hearse. Two of them. The wife, the kids, a boyfriend; his sisters, the brother from Australia. They watched as they all got out of the cars and the undertaker's men took the coffin from the back of the hearse and carried it into the church.

He and Lizzie went about halfway up the aisle, not too near, not too far back. Martin hadn't been in the church in years. But he remembered it exactly, how cold it always was. How far down his knees would have to go before they landed on the padding that ran under the back of the seat in front of him, when the priest told them to kneel. How Jesus in the Stations of the Cross looked a bit like Keith Richards. He was going to show Lizzie, to remind her.

But he heard the gasp. That was what it sounded like, the whole place gasping, softly, everybody there. He looked. Noel's wife was walking away from the coffin. She'd put a framed photograph on top of it.

Noel. That was what the gasp was for. Noel, twenty-five years before.

—Jesus. Look at that.

He'd forgotten. He'd forgotten that Noel used to look like that. A big man with a big grin and a big collar on his red shirt. A big handsome man. A young man, looking back at the camera. Right into his future.

He'd forgotten. The last two years, they'd watched Noel get smaller. And, in the last months, the smaller version became the man. The man Martin hoped he wasn't talking to for the last time. He'd looked at him carefully, already remembering, storing him away. And he'd forgotten about the real man. The full man. But there he was now, on the coffin.

It should have been heartbreaking. And it was. Seeing the faded colour, the big collar. He felt guilty. He'd let himself forget. He'd let the sick man become the man. He'd forgotten why Noel had been Noel, why they'd been friends. But there was more – the guilt didn't settle.

He could feel it, and hear. The gasp had become whispers. The photograph. Noel's wife – Barbara – her putting the picture there, on the coffin, that was brilliant. And brave – going up there, letting the wood of the frame clatter against the coffin lid. Keeping her hands steady. She was even smiling when she came back and sat down.

Martin could see Davie in front of him, and the other men he knew and liked, all looking at each other, over other people's heads, smiling. *Sad* and *good* had become the same thing. Martin wanted to talk. He wanted to laugh. He wanted to stop being the man with diverticular disease. He felt Lizzie beside him. He nudged her knee with his. She nudged back.

The priest was walking over to the platform beside the altar, and the microphone. Martin heard a soft voice somewhere behind him, a man.

—Here goes.

They stood.

Teaching

—You know my mother.

The girl stood beside his desk. She was one of those big-eyed kids. She'd always look a bit like a kid. By the time she was thirty-five, she'd be a strange-looking kid.

—You know my mother, she said again.

Now though, she was one of those lovely kids. She'd stopped, hesitated, on her way past his desk to the door. One of the last out. She'd probably made sure of that. It was her first full day in the secondary school.

He finished what he was doing. Searching for a red biro at the bottom of his bag. And he looked at her.

—Is that right? he said.

—Yeah.

He looked for her mother in the kid's face.

Big eyes. He stopped looking. He could feel the sweat on his forehead.

—Who is she? he said.

—Amanda Collins, she said.

—Amanda Collins?

—Yeah. Do you remember her?

—I do, yeah.

But he didn't.

—How is she?

—She's grand, said the kid.

—Good.

—She says they all fancied you.

She wasn't the first. The last five or six years, kids had been stopping at his desk. Their first day, their big news. You knew my ma or my da.

This was killing him.

It was getting harder. Getting through the day, the nine class periods. It was the first week in September.

She was still there. He'd have to say something. Silence wouldn't work.

—It's hard to imagine, he said. —Isn't it?

—Yeah.

He looked at her. He laughed – relief. He couldn't believe he'd been so stupid. Even as he heard himself say it. Like some seedy old man, flirting or something.

She laughed too. A lovely kid. Open. Like her mother must have been. Why he'd loved teaching, when he'd started, and for a long time afterwards.

He didn't drink in the day. His head was telling him he should, something quick to swallow the headache. But he didn't. He never had and he never would. There was no flask or bottle in his bag. No quick dash down to the local. Too many parents, too much self-respect.

He used to like it, kids stopping for a chat. *What*

groups are you into, sir? Our cat's after having kittens. D'you want one, sir? Things like that. He used to write down the best of them.

It didn't really happen now. Kids didn't stop. He wrote down nothing.

The kid here was going.

—See you tomorrow, sir.

He looked at his timetable. It was open, on his desk.

—Yes, he said.—Tomorrow. Bye.

—Bye.

She left the door open. A lovely kid. He'd smile every time she walked in, for the next six years.

He went to the door. He used to stand there between classes and watch the world go by. All those tall and tiny children. More than a thousand of them on the move. He could have named most of them. He shut the door.

Things changed. It wasn't just him. He wasn't denying anything: his heart wasn't in it. He wished he was somewhere else. But there weren't as many students now; the area outside was changing. The corridor wasn't as packed as it had been when he'd started, twenty-three years before.

He looked again at the timetable. He sat down. He had to bring the page closer to his eyes. He didn't have a class now; he was free till eleven o'clock.

It wasn't just him. Something had happened. A kid stopping at the desk, a boy or a girl, had become something to be wary of, almost to dread. They'd been given talks, in the staffroom, on the telltale signs – the eyes,

31

marks, cuts. He was probably the only member of staff left who hadn't been told an abuse story. He'd expected it to happen. For a long time. He'd felt left out when it didn't. He'd even been ready to make up something, when a gang of the teachers had gone for an impromptu pint after work. The urge to tell, to get back his status as one of the nice teachers. But he'd been wise; he'd kept his mouth shut.

He looked at the timetable again. He had two classes left to lunchtime, and another two after. That wasn't too bad. He looked at his watch. The headache was starting to lift. He'd be better in the next class; he'd get up and move around. He'd be Robin Williams for half an hour, in *Dead Poets Society*. One of those Seize the Day classes. The way he used to be, all day. He'd even said it once. *Seize the day, boys and girls*. They'd cheered.

He had an abuse story of his own. He'd been in First Year, like the big-eyed kid who'd just left. A few months in the new school, and he knew hardly anyone. He'd been sent to the Christian Brothers and he still hadn't got used to them. They were strange men, sometimes funny, but savage and unpredictable. The lay teachers were as bad. If he listened, he could hear shouting or crying, someone being hit, in another part of the building. The noises were always hanging there. Once, he remembered, a boy in the room next door was thrown against the classroom wall, and he watched the blackboard on his side come off its hinges and fall to the wooden floor. They'd laughed. They'd all laughed. They'd laughed at everything.

There was one of the brothers, Brother Flynn. Latin and civics. He'd stand at the front of the room and smile and rub his big hands. But he could just as easily bring the hands down on someone's head, one onto each ear. The front desk was a death sentence. But, really, Flynn was alright. He was the only teacher who used their first names. He didn't go mad when he saw the names of English football teams on the covers of their books and copies. Flynn was a laugh.

But Flynn liked him. He'd smile at him when he was testing their Latin vocabulary. The others noticed.

—Smile back and he won't give us any homework.

—Lay off.

—Go on, yeh queer.

—Fuck off.

Flynn patted his shoulder one day as he was going past. He wanted to cry. He wanted to get out the window, drop to the ground, run into the sea across the road. He knew the others were looking. He knew they'd be waiting to get him when the bell went and Flynn left the room. He hated Flynn and he needed him in the room.

It had only lasted for a while. He got to know a few of the other lads. They got the same bus home; he made them laugh. They knew he was sound, and soon the stuff about Flynn became a joke. He was one of them now, so he wasn't a queer. Flynn still smiled, and it didn't matter.

Then he was sick. One morning, he felt hot. His forehead, his whole face, was suddenly wet with sweat. He put his hand up.

—Brother!

He was going to puke. Flynn must have noticed, must have seen the colour dropping off his face. He opened the door.

—Quick, quick!

Flynn was standing outside when he came back out of the toilet. He smiled at him. He said he'd drive him home. He told Flynn that his mother wouldn't be there; she went to his granny's on Mondays, two buses across the city.

Flynn took him over to the house where all the Brothers lived, beside the school. He'd never been in the house before. He'd never really been near it. It was a rule that never had to be remembered: don't go near the Brothers' house. Water dripped from the roof of the porch onto the red and black tiles.

—Mind you don't slip, said Flynn.

He remembered shivering, remembered feeling the cold on his skin.

Flynn opened the front door. He followed him into the hall. The same red and black tiles.

—Shut the door.

He pushed the front door closed. The lock was colossal, a big black box screwed right into the wood.

Flynn kept walking. He stood for a while, then followed him. Flynn's black shoes on the tiles, and his own shoes – they were the only noises. The house was empty. He'd seen the housekeeper once, a woman much older than his mother, walking towards the Brothers' house with a net shopping bag full of apples. But she wasn't there now. He could tell – something about the cold: the house had been empty for hours.

Flynn pulled open a door. He disappeared behind it, then came back out, backwards. He was dragging something. It was a fold-up bed, on castors. The castors squealed across the tiles. Flynn dragged the bed across the hall, to another door. He stayed where he was. Flynn was still going backwards, pulling the bed, looking at him.

—Come on, he said.

He didn't move. He remembered that. He remembered the slow terror, in his legs.

—Come on, said Flynn.—Quick now.

He watched, stayed at the door, as Flynn unfolded the bed. He heard him grunt as he pushed the two sides down. It was the dining room, or something. Flynn pushed the bed against the long table.

—There you are. Lie down.

Flynn walked across to the window. He heard him pull the curtains. It didn't make the room much darker. He sat down on the bed. It moved a bit, on the castors. He took off his shoes. He stood up again. He could hear Flynn's feet. He pulled back the grey blanket. The mattress was bare, and striped.

He lay down. He felt the bed move under him again, just a bit, an inch. He pulled the blanket over his chest. The room got darker. Flynn was standing in front of the light coming from the hall.

—How's the tummy now?

—Alright, Brother.

—Are you going to be sick again, d'you think?

35

—No, Brother.

He felt the blanket being pulled away from him, but he couldn't see Flynn's hands. Then he saw Flynn's face, close to his own. He was leaning over him. The blanket was gone. Then it was back; he felt it land on his legs, his waist, his chest. He felt Flynn's hands at his neck. He could feel Flynn's knuckles, on his chin. Flynn was holding the blanket. He was tucking it under his neck. He was looking down at him. He was smiling.

That was it, all he could remember. He half expected more to open up – the hand grabbing his neck, holding him down – but it never did. He'd told someone about it once, a woman at a party. He'd stopped where his memory stopped, at the man tucking the blanket under the boy's chin. He was sitting beside the woman, two kitchen chairs side by side. She looked at him, then told him that he was an apologist for the Catholic Church. She stood up as she said it.

There was something, colour, at the corner of his eye. He glanced over at the classroom door. The principal was looking in the window. She waved, and went. He looked down at his desk. What had she seen? His diary was open, so was one of his books. His timetable. His pen was there as well. It was fine. He was working. He felt his face. He'd shaved that morning.

Not that it mattered. It had never mattered, that kind of idiocy, in this school. How you taught, not how you dressed; that was what mattered. It was one of the things he'd loved about the place. But he'd noticed. His beard had changed colour. There was grey in it, even a bit of white. He looked like a wino or something if he didn't shave every second day.

The principal was younger than he was. She'd come to the school four years after he had. He'd kissed her once – he cringed; he looked at the window.

He looked at his timetable. It was darker in the room now; it was going to rain. This had been his room for more than twenty years. He knew the light and every noise.

He'd do something about the drinking. He'd give it up. He would – he could. He'd watched a football match the night before, the Champions League, on RTE, the whole thing. But he didn't know who'd played. He remembered nothing. Not a thing. He'd have to read the report in the paper before lunch; the paper was in his bag. Then he'd be able to talk about it, if he talked to anyone. But he'd probably stay in the room. Plan his classes.

He'd stop. The drinking. He wasn't fooling himself. He knew it was serious.

He'd kissed her. That first year she'd been in the school. After a union meeting.

He smiled. The absurdity. The idea of kissing her now. He looked at the window in the door. There was no one there. He looked at the timetable. Sixth Year English was next. A double class, Ordinary level. There were no Honours classes on his timetable. It was five years since he'd had an Honours class. Nothing had been said.

These kids were fine. He'd had them last year. But there was no life in them. He'd have sworn it was true. It just wasn't like it used to be.

He wrote in his diary: NOVEL. He'd do the novel with them, a good start to the year. What novel was it? Had they done it already, last year? He looked at his shelf. He knew all the books, the shapes, the colours of the spines; he didn't have to read the titles. Which one was it?

He'd do something else with them. He'd think of something. He was good at that. Seize the day. The spontaneity. Not with this gang, though. Those days were over. He'd have to have something ready.

He stood up. His knee cracked. Something dry in the joint. He went to the bookshelf.

That was something he definitely remembered – the first time he'd heard his knee crack. It was the last time he'd been with a woman, and sober enough to remember it.

—What was that?

She'd thought it was an animal or something, under the bed. Gnawing a bone. She'd made him turn on the light. A disaster, the two of them. Squinting – reality. He got off the bed and heard the crack again.

—My knee, he said.

—What?

—The noise, he said.—Listen.

He moved again. She heard the crack. She started crying. A disaster.

He still liked the teaching. He hadn't changed that much. He liked the new kids who were beginning to turn up every year, the sons and daughters of the immigrants. Black kids with Dublin accents. And the East Europeans. Lovely kids. And it reminded him – now; he could feel it – of why he'd loved teaching. Empowerment. He'd loved that word. He'd believed it. Giving power to working-class kids. He could get worked up about poverty, and why he was there in the school. A word like 'underclass' could still get him going, the convenience and cynicism of it. Hiding all that social injustice and inequality in a word like that. The working class became the underclass, and their problems became inevitable. His thinking hadn't changed. When he thought.

He looked at his watch. He had twenty minutes left. There was a tiny crack in the glass, and a line of mist at the crack, under the glass. He'd no idea when that had happened.

There'd been one woman. She'd said it once: she loved the way he thought.

He had an address in his wallet. AA. The address and the times. Alcoholics Anonymous. It was in his jacket, in the inside pocket, ready for whenever he wanted it. Someone had given it to him. A cousin of his. At his uncle's funeral, at the few drinks after the burial. He didn't get it at first; he didn't know what she was doing. He thought she was slipping him her phone number and he was running through the ethics and legality of it, phoning his own cousin, arranging to meet for a date – because she wasn't a bad-looking woman and, really, he hardly knew her. He hadn't seen her since they were kids. But it hadn't been her number at all. It was an address for Alcoholics Anonymous, and the meeting times. He'd thought about going, to see if she'd be there. But he hadn't gone. He hadn't wanted to; he hadn't felt the need. Still, he'd held onto the address. He knew it was there.

He looked at his watch. He had thirteen minutes, plenty of time. He'd give them the opening sentence of a story, and get them to continue. That always worked. He'd give them a good one.

He'd come close once, with a woman. Mary. They'd been together for two years. He'd just graduated, started teaching. She was still in her final year. She'd be finished in August, and he knew what would happen then. She'd get a teaching job like his. Their salaries would meet and they'd buy a house and get married. Because her mother would deliver The Great Silence until they did. They laughed about it, The Great Silence, her name for the mother's war against any urges or opinions that might deflect her children from their proper course: the career, the four-bedroom house, the husband or wife, the happiness that was Southside, Catholic respectability. They laughed but they'd known: the old bitch would win. They'd never admit it, the choices would be theirs – but they'd do it. They'd get the mortgage; it was mad to carry on renting. They'd get married; for tax reasons. In a church; for the laugh. They'd known – *he'd* known. And he'd done the right thing. He sat beside her and told her it was over. He remembered the elation as he left her in the pub and went back to their flat, to pack. Throwing everything into two bags. Going. There'd been a few phone calls, then that was it. He was alone. He could live.

One night, a few years ago, he'd been watching a current affairs programme on RTE, after the News. He was only half watching, and reading. He looked up at the screen. He recognised her before he remembered her name. Mary. She was in some city in Africa and she was talking to people – children and women – who'd been deported from Ireland, interviewing them. In small, dark rooms, or rooms that seemed to be missing walls, that were sliding onto the street.

He watched. She stood on a street that looked like the scene of recent violence and spoke to the camera. There were two men with rifles just behind her. She looked well. She looked great. The report ended.

He had seven minutes. *Seize the day, boys and girls.* Teaching was a branch of show business. He'd always said it. Grab the kids and bring them with you. Empowerment. He stood at the board. He waited for the idea, the opening sentence that they'd read on their way into the room, the sentence that would have them grabbing their pens and folders from their bags. He hadn't eaten in days; he wasn't hungry. But he thought that food, anything, might help with the headache.

But there was his idea. He wrote it on the board. 'He hadn't eaten in days.' He looked at it.

Six minutes.

He sat down. He was pleased. He was sorted, organised, up to lunchtime. Only nine more months to go. He made himself smile. He was back on track. He opened his diary again, put it beside his timetable. He'd plan ahead. He'd memorise the students' names. He'd smile at them when they came into the room. He'd chat to them. He'd bring them with him. Empowerment. It was still there; he could feel it, across his chest. He wouldn't drink today; he'd go straight home. He'd get food on the way. He'd get some new clothes at the weekend. He'd go to a film or a play.

That big-eyed kid, the one who'd told him that he'd known her mother. He wished that kid was his. It was ridiculous – the thought just rolled through him. Brother Flynn – the man's smile, looking down at him. He wanted to look at someone that way, to smile down at his own child. To be able to do it. Whatever it took, whatever he gave up or didn't give up.

It was ridiculous.

He stood up. He opened the door. He was ready for the bell. He looked at the board. 'He hadn't eaten in days.' They'd love that. Kidnapping, starvation; the boys would love it. But he had another idea. He went back to the board and picked up the chalk. He wrote under the first sentence: 'She hadn't eaten in days.' That was even better. They could have the choice. He could feel it in him. It was the old feeling, back. The hands would be up, asking him how to spell 'anorexia'. He could already feel the buzz, the energy. He'd stay standing, walk among them. He'd smile. He'd laugh.

He looked at his watch.

One minute.

He was fine.

The Slave

My very educated mother just showed us nine planets. My very educated mother just showed us nine planets. My, Mercury. Very, Venus. Educated, Earth. Mother, Mars. Just, Jupiter. Showed, Saturn. Us, Uranus. Nine, Neptune. Planets, Pluto. All of them, in the right order. It was brilliant. The only problem was the two Ms, Mercury and Mars. Mixing them up. Except for that, it was plain sailing. Simple. That was what I liked about it. All that complicated business straightened and tidied into one sentence. Even if the sentence itself was stupid. My very educated mother. Just showed us nine planets. Mind you, that bit is good. Because there *are* nine of them. So it fits and helps you remember.

And it's about the only thing I remember learning in school. I must have learnt more, I'm not saying that. A lot more, actually. I can read, for fuck sake. I'm a two books a week man; I eat the fuckin' things. So, yeah. But I don't remember learning how to read. And I do remember my very educated mother. Like it was now. The first week of secondary school. And the teacher, God love her. Miss something. O'Keefe, I think it was. Something like that. Her name was on the timetable, 'O'Whatever it was. Miss.' We were hoping a nice bit of stuff would come walking in the door. But in marches your woman. Older than our ma's, as ugly as our da's. With a box of chalk. Holding it up in the air, like a cup or something, a trophy. And she waits till there's absolute silence.

—What is this? she says, and she points at some poor cunt at the front. Me.

—A box of chalk, I say, and wait to be told I'm wrong.

But —Yes, she says.—It *is* a box of chalk. And what type of chalk is it?

I look at the box.

—Coloured, I say, and I'm right again. Twice in a row, for the first time in my life. And the last.

—Yes, she says.—It is coloured chalk. And it is mine.

She goes over to the desk. The teacher's desk, like, the one at the front. She opens the drawer and in goes the chalk.

—I am Miss – whatever it is, she says.—And I am your geography teacher. We will meet three times a week. And three times a week I will open this drawer and I will find my chalk exactly as I left it. I have information to impart but I cannot do this to my satisfaction if I do not have my coloured chalk.

And then she says – you've guessed it.—Do I make myself clear?

—Yes, Miss, say the saps at the front, *mise** here included.

—A stick of coloured chalk is the geography teacher's essential tool, she says.—The box contains ten sticks and it will contain ten sticks when we meet again on Wednesday.

'Wed-nesday', she called it. Some hope, the poor eejit. The other teachers took it, every fuckin' stick. It was all gone by lunchtime.

Anyway, she took a stick of ordinary white off the tray at the bottom of the blackboard, and then she wrote my very educated mother, down the board instead of across, and the names of the planets that the words stood for beside them. And I've remembered it ever since, and nothing else. Precious little. The only other thing I remember clearly is the Latin teacher. I did Latin, believe it or not. And I remember none of it. But I *do* remember him. He went around the room every morning, putting his hand down our jumpers to make sure we were wearing vests. A Christian Brother he was, and I can remember *his* name. But I'll keep it to myself. Yeah, I remember him, alright. Every morning, right through the winter. Feeling my chest. Leaving his hand there forever. Freezing. Rough palms – old cuts gone hard, years of swinging a hurley. That was my only experience of abuse. His hand. He's still alive as well. So I'm told. I should report him, I suppose. Only, (a) I don't think I could handle the humiliation, and (b) I'd hate

* *Mise* ('mish-eh') – me.

45

anyone to know that I used to wear a vest. And it's harmless enough when you hear about some of the other things that went on. And he did it to all of us; he wasn't just picking on me.

But no, I can't remember a word of Latin. And I'm not blaming the Brother, mind. Not at all. I've no French either, barely a word. Maths, history – tiny bits, only. 1916. 1798. Black '47. Irish? Ah, goodnight. *Oíche mhaith.*† I can hardly help the kids with their home-work and the eldest left me behind years ago. No, the only thing I remember, consciously remember, is that thing, my very educated mother. But she was a clown, the teacher. We ate the poor woman after we got the hang of her.

—Is there life on Uranus, Miss?

—No, indeed.

She was fierce enough that first day, with her box of chalk. Scary. Worthy of a bit of respect. But then, I suppose it was when she said about the chalk being her essential tool, we realised then she was just a mad ol' bitch and we made her life a misery.

But. It has to be said. She taught me the only thing I remember. And it's not just that I remember it now and again, when I hear one of the words, say, 'mother' or 'very', or there's something on the telly about astronomy. I remember it every day. It's not a memory, no more than the names of my children are. One of your kids comes running up to you with its head split open, you

† *Oíche mhaith* ('ee-heh wah') – goodnight.

don't have to think of its name. The names are always there. And it's the same with my very educated mother.

It's like this. Every day, I walk down to the Dart station – like I'll do this morning. I'm on a job in town. Have been for the last six months, and there's another year in it, I'd say. With a bit of luck. So I leave the tools in a strongbox on the job and I don't bother with the van. I walk down to the station, and there's a bit of a hill just before it and when I get to the top there's the Pigeon House chimneys in front of me. God's socks, the eldest used to call them. In the days when she used to talk to us. And every time, *every* time I hit the top of the hill it goes through my head, the same thing: my very educated mother. Don't ask me why, but it's like clockwork. I don't expect it or anticipate it. It just pops into my head. And it stays lodged in there until I get to the station. Every morning. Rain, wind or hail.

And that was what went through my head the morning I found the rat.

I shut the kitchen door. And I leaned back against it. I had to force myself to breathe. To remember – to *breathe*. In, out. In, out. My heart was pounding, Jesus, like the worst hangover I'd ever had. It was sore. Really sore, now – like a heart attack. Huge in my chest. And I leaned against the kitchen door.

Just out there, out in the hall. In, out. In, out. My very educated mother. My very educated mother. And when I got the breathing together, I went back in. I went in and I had another look, to make sure I'd actually seen what I'd seen. I was half sure there'd be nothing there.

47

It was a bit of brown paper, a wrapper or something, one of the baby's furry toys. Or even nothing at all. A shadow. It was just about dawn, the blinds were open. Any of the things on the windowsill could have made a shadow. At that hour of the morning. I took the long way. Instead of going straight for the fridge, the direct route. I came around here, to this side of the counter. I was scared, yeah. I'm not going to *not* admit that. But I wanted to *see*, to be absolutely sure. To see it from a distance and an angle. To be absolutely positive.

And, yeah, it was there. In under the pull-out larder. A rat. A dead fuckin' rat. A huge fucker.

Lying there.

And I still couldn't accept it. I couldn't – comprehend it. I was staring at the fuckin' thing. There was nothing else, in my head, in the world, just that thing lying there, under my pull-out larder, that I installed myself – that was my own fuckin' idea – and I couldn't get to grips with the situation. I couldn't just say to myself,—That's a rat there, Terry, and you'd want to think about getting rid of it.

No. I couldn't organise myself. I couldn't *think*. I walked out and shut the door again. I was going to go back in and go through it all over again.

And then I heard him. The baby. Inside in the sitting room.

And I kind of cracked up.

It was only a few inches from my feet; did I tell you that? Yeah. Two, three inches. Making the coffee, I was. Good, strong coffee. I picked up the habit in America, in Florida, on the holliers. Orlando. Before the baby. He was conceived there, actually, now that I think of it. During a storm. Thunder, lightning. It was something else; you'd never see it here. And good music on the radio at the same time. Good seventies stuff, you know. *On a dark desert highway, cool wind in my hair*. It all seemed to fit. The music and the weather. Even though it was pissing outside and he was singing about the desert. But it was American. And we were *there*. Myself and herself, after all those years. And that kind of explains why we've one child that's eight years younger than the others. He's a souvenir, God love him. Him and the coffee.

Anyway, I'm making the coffee. I've done the plunger bit and I've gone to the fridge for the milk. I drop the spoon, and I'm halfway down to picking it up when I see it. The fuckin' spoon was right beside it. It's probably the first time I ever dropped a spoon in my life. I *don't* drop things.

Anyway, I'm leaning against the kitchen door and I hear the baby chatting to himself in the sitting room. That's when I get really upset. I'm nearly crying, I don't mind admitting it. But I'm also thinking, and I'm straight back into the kitchen. I'm thinking, deciding.

—Terry, I'm saying, out loud for all I know.—Action stations. Let's get rid of the cunt. Gloves and bag. Gloves and bag.

I shut the door behind me, to make sure himself doesn't come in and see it on the floor or me with it in my hand. I go over to the press where she keeps the plastic bags.

She's mad into the environment, dead keen. We've a whole house full of plastic bags. Anyway, so far, so good. I'm doing something. I'm in control. The press is over there. The one under the sink. Well away from your man on the floor. There's no need for me to go too near him yet. I'm assuming he was a male. It's hard to imagine that there'd be such a thing as a female rat. But that's just me being stupid. Let's just say it was a male; it's easier for me. I had go past him, whatever sex he was. But I didn't have to look at him, to get to the sink. I go straight over and I have the door open before it dawns on me that he might have friends in the vicinity. Fuckin' hell, I nearly shat myself; I nearly fell into the press. But it was empty; it was grand. No sign of disorder, claws, droppings – it was grand. I take out four of the bags. There's hundreds of them in there. And one of the big black bin ones. I shake out the bags and put them on the counter, one, and one, and one, and the last one. Really fast now, no procrastinating. No way. Not with the baby in the room next door.

That's the problem, to an extent. He's not a baby, really. Not any more. He stood up about a year ago, without bothering to crawl first. Up he gets, using the couch and my leg to hoist himself, and he's been flying around the place ever since, except when he falls over asleep. We just call him the baby. He'll probably be the last, so he'll b the baby for a while yet. Even though he's built like a shithouse and he'll probably be shaving before the end of the year, the speed he's growing. He'll be the last, I'd say. She swings a bit but I'm fairly certain.

So, on with the gloves. Yellow Marigolds, way too small for me. I have to force them on but the only alternative is picking him up with my bare hands and that possibility doesn't even occur to me. So, I'm all set. I turn to face him. But, God, I feel very exposed. I'm only in my dressing gown. This one here is new, from herself for the anniversary. Eighteen years. I got her a brooch. Doesn't sound like much but it's very nice.

Anyway, it wasn't really the dressing gown. It was the feet. I was in my bare feet. I hadn't bought these yokes here yet. The slippers. I know the rat was dead and not particularly interested in biting my toe or having a look under my dressing gown. But, still, I didn't feel ready for battle. Even if the enemy was dead and stiff. I hated myself then. That was the lowest, really. I couldn't move. I couldn't do what I was supposed to do. I stared down at your man on the floor. In under the pull-out. He was lying on his side. No teeth showing, no grimace, you know, nothing like agony or anger. He was just quietly dead. But I couldn't bend down and pick him up. I just couldn't do it. My home, my pull-out, my family, my little son next door in the sitting room, this bastard had come into my home – *how* is another story – and I couldn't just bend down, pick the cunt up and throw him in a bag.

I really let myself down.

Then I did it.

Just like that. I bent down. I put my hand around him. He was stiff, solid, like wood or metal with a bit of weight on it. Or one of those Transformers toys, but heavier. And I could feel him, even with the gloves on. Cold. Cold and hard. I couldn't feel the hair, thank God. I dropped him into the first plastic bag. And I tied it at the top. Into the next bag, and the next one, and the next, and into the black bag. Then I took him out to the shed. It was cold out there, and still a bit dark, like now. But I still did it, in my bare feet. Just to have him properly out of the way. And I came back in here.

And then – and I'm a bit proud of this – I decided to go ahead with my coffee. Mission accomplished, the worst was over. I'd just carried a dead rat from here to there. I'd sorted out the problem, done what I was supposed to do. I opened the kitchen door again, and I realised that I was still wearing the rubber gloves. So I was taking them off and deciding what to do with them when he came in looking for his breakfast.

And that, I suppose, is what really got me thinking. Really thinking. Not just reacting to the crisis, getting rid of the rat. It went beyond the rat. The rat isn't really involved.

That's my arse. Of course the rat's involved. The rat's to blame.

It's hard to explain.

Look. I never owned a pair of slippers in my life. Now, I fuckin' need them. I got these ones in Clery's. They're alright. They're grand. But I never wanted them. I never fuckin' wanted them. I never wanted to be a man who wore slippers. I always liked the feel of the house under my feet. Get into a pair of slippers and you're fucked; your life is over. That's what I've always felt,

52

since I was a teenager and my father got a pair from our granny and he put them on, sat down in his chair in the corner and never got up again. I mean, he did get up. He went to work, he went into the kitchen and up to the jacks. But that was it: he was old. It got to the point where he wouldn't say hello when he came home from work. He wouldn't acknowledge the family, my mother, until after his feet were safe inside the slippers. We weren't getting on at the time. A bit like me and my eldest now, actually. And everything I hated about him, about myself, about everything, I aimed at those slippers. And now here's me, after buying my own slippers. I've no one to blame but myself. And the rat.

But it's not just the rat and the slippers. Not really. Look it, I'm forty-two. I don't mind. I was forty-one last year, I'll be forty-three next year. I'm not the worst-looking man in the world. There are lads that work with me ten years younger, and they're in bits. I'm Leonardo DiCaprio standing beside some of those cunts.

And I read. I'm interested in the world. I still get excited about things. I still love watching her brushing her teeth, for example. I still want to go over and clean her mouth out with my tongue, just like I wanted to, and did, from day one. And she still knows it. And other things too.

But I'm forty-two. I'm middle-aged. That's a mathematical fact. In fact, more than half my life is over. So my eldest told me, which was fuckin' charming. The last time she said anything to me. Something about statistics they were doing in school. But, really, it was because

53

I won't let her watch *Trainspotting*. It's a good film but she's still too young. That was what I told her. Next year, probably. Which I thought was reasonable. It's a good film, like I said. But there's too much in it that's not – okay, suitable. Unfortunately, that was the word I used. 'Suitable.' Her face, Jesus. It hurt. Maybe I'm just being stupid; I don't know. She's nearly seventeen. Anyway, that was when she informed me that my life was more than half over.

But that's not the point. Middle age. The midlife crisis. Whatever you want to call it. I was forty-two when I saw the rat. I'd still be forty-two if I'd never seen it. Okay, I'm after getting myself a pair of slippers but I don't believe that they have evil powers. They haven't made me grow old all of the sudden.

No.

What has really rattled me, what has changed my life, to the extent that it'll probably never be the same again, is the question that came into my head when the little lad came into the kitchen wanting his breakfast.

—Cry-babies, he says.

That's what he calls Rice Krispies. It'd break your heart. Bright as a button.

—Cry-babies, Dada.

And me trying to take off the rubber gloves.

What if?

That was it.

What if. What if he'd been the first one to come into the kitchen? What if he'd picked it up? What if it hadn't been dead? It goes on and on, backwards and forwards, right through everything. There's no end to it. It won't go away and it's not going to go away, and I don't know if I can cope.

I've never been a great sleeper. I don't know about when I was a kid. I don't remember. I suppose I was normal. But since then, especially in the last few years, I've got by on very little. Even in the days when I drank a bit, I still got up early, even when my head was hopping. I never liked lying in bed. I'd go down to the kitchen and stick my mouth under the cold tap until I could feel the water negotiating with the hangover. That was as much of a cure as I needed, until a few years ago and I began to feel it a bit more. I've always managed on four or five hours' sleep. And I rarely feel the lack.

I don't drink at all now. I gave up a couple of years back. I just gave up; nothing dramatic. I'd no real taste for it any more. Not that I was a big drinker. Just the three or four pints. That was what I settled down to after I got married and the kids started arriving. Not every night either; a couple of times a week. Then once a week. And then I stopped going altogether. I got lazy. I'd go down to the local and the lads I knew, the ones I really liked, wouldn't be there. They'd gotten lazy like me, I suppose, and there was one of them died. The hangovers, with the kids and that, they just weren't worth it any more. Especially when the lads stopped coming down – after Frankie died, really. Enough was enough. If we go out for a meal, me and her, I'll have a glass of wine but I'm just as happy with a 7-UP.

But back to the sleep thing. The night after I found the rat, I slept as much and as well as I usually do. I just slept. I didn't dream about rats, as far as I know, and I didn't wake up screaming. I just woke up. As usual. I felt a bit robbed, as usual, with the feeling that I could have done with an extra half-hour. I grabbed the book from beside the bed and got up. I went through the whole routine, exactly as I'd done the morning before and every morning before that, going back years.

But it was different. There was the world of difference. I turned on the lights as I came down, which I usually wouldn't have done. But you'd expect that, after the shock I'd had the day before. I gave the door over there an almighty clatter before I came in. Again, that's only to be expected. Even though I knew there were no more rats. The pest control lads had given the place a good going-over the day before. I'd had to go to work but she told me all about it when I got home and when I'd phoned her earlier during the day.

—They're up in the attic, looking for droppings, she says when I phoned her the first time.—Nice enough fellas.

As calm as anything. It annoyed me a bit. The thing didn't get to her the same way it got to me. Mind you, to be fair to her, she never saw the fuckin' thing. And, to be fair to me, I did. Anyway, by the time I got home she was an expert on rats and mice. The world's foremost fuckin' expert. No, that's not fair.

Anyway.

—They're neophobic, she says after I said I'd go up

the attic to see if the poison had been touched yet.—They're scared of anything new, she says, even though I could have worked it out myself.—So there's no point going up. They won't touch it for a few days, until they're used to it being there.

All I'd wanted to do was prove that I wasn't too scared to go up. I just wanted to do something useful, after running off to work earlier and leaving her flicking through the Golden Pages.

—Did they take the rat with them? I said.

—What rat? she says.

—The rat, I said.—The fuckin' rat I found this morning.

—Oh, she said.—No.

So that's what I did. I got rid of the rat. I went for a walk. With the black bag. No bother. I went looking for a skip. And there was one just up the road. So, into the skip with the fucker in the black bag. I shoved it down under some of the rubble, to make sure no kids pulled it out and started messing with it. I could feel it under the layers of plastic and I didn't mind a bit.

But that's not the point. The point is – I don't know, exactly. What I used to take for granted, I can't take for granted any more. I used to be able to walk across the floor here without giving it a moment's thought. And now I can't. I have to think about it. I have to prepare myself. I have to casually search the floor. I have to get down on my knees and check under the presses, knowing I'll find nothing. My mornings are ruined. It's as simple as that.

But there's more to it than that. It's the 'what if' thing. That's the real point. What if it had been Sunday morning, early, and *Match of the Day* had been on. I'd have sat down to have a look because I hardly ever watch it on Saturday nights any more. It's hard to get worked up about millionaires half your age. Not that I begrudge them the money. Anyway, I'd have sat down and the little lad would have strolled on into the kitchen. It doesn't bear thinking about. But I've thought about nothing else. And it goes way beyond that. Everything. Fuckin' everything is *polluted* by it.

I wait up every night when the eldest goes out, till she comes home. And I was just getting used to it. I was capable of falling asleep before she came home. I'd wake up when I'd hear her key in the latch, but I'd be back in bed, not an embarrassment to her, before I'd hear her feet on the stairs. Now, Jesus. Last Saturday I sat on the stairs, in the dark. I know – like any normal father. But it isn't. It's desperate. I had to nail myself to the stairs to stop from going out to the street or driving to the disco, or whatever it's called – the club she said she was going to. It's not that I don't trust her. I don't. But I do, if that makes sense.

It makes perfect sense. I trust her. I'm happy, *was* happy to let her out, to have her own key and the rest of it. And I'm absolutely positive she abuses that trust. She drinks. I know. She might even be doing the Ecstasy and that. And, yeah, sex, I suppose. And I really don't mind because that's part of the package as well. Part of the contract, giving her a longer leash. And as long as she doesn't stroll into the house with a smell of drink on her and say, 'Sorry I'm late, I was riding a chap with a car and a ponytail,' I don't mind. What isn't said didn't happen. She knows; we know. She's finding her feet. We're here if she needs us.

But *now*, fuck. I'm on the verge of giving out to her because she looks good. As if she's to blame for being an attractive young one, as if it's anything to blame anyone for. I was never like that. I was always proud of her, always. But now I'm terrified. I remember the first time we let her go down to the shops by herself. It was a real event, that day. She was so proud of herself, you know. She was just eight. I've always loved that, giving them the opportunity to be proud of themselves. If it was now though, I wouldn't let it happen.

Anyway.

She – my wife. Jackie. She's worried about me. Which is about the only thing going for me at the moment. It proves something – I don't know what. Love, I suppose. I see her looking at me and I want to shout at her to leave me alone but I'm grateful for it as well.

I don't know anything any more. I don't seem to. I'm getting pains in my chest. And my arms are stiff when I wake up. Numb. I remember in a film I saw when I was a kid, *The Birdman of Alcatraz*, the warden, your man from *The Streets of San Francisco* – not Michael Douglas, the other one. Your man with the nose. Karl something. He had a pain in his arm – Karl Malden – and Burt Lancaster, the birdman, knew that he was going to have a heart attack. I remember being fascinated by that, that a pain in your arm was a sign that there was something wrong with your heart. It was great. And my father, of course, he wanted to know if a pain in your arse meant you were going to have a brain haemorrhage. This was before he got the slippers. But anyway. What do two numb arms mean? Two heart attacks?

I don't give a fuck about anything any more. I really don't. I'm reading this one here. *Cold Mountain* by Charles Frazier. It's good, you know. It's very good. And I couldn't care less. I'm reading it because it's what I do. I'm just doing it. But I don't care. She used to like that about me, the opposite, you know. She always said it. My enthusiasm. She loved the way I listened to music. I leaned into it. I really listened. I never noticed, but she did. And it was the same with books, and everything really. There was once she made me read in bed, out loud, while she got on top of me, and I read right up to the second before I came. It wasn't easy, hanging on to the right page. It wasn't a hardback, thank Jesus. *The Slave*, by Isaac Bashevis Singer. What a book that was. I'd never read anything like it before. Or since. It made me regret that I wasn't a Jew, because of the way the main lad, Jacob, struggled to hold on to his Jewishness all through the book. He was the slave in the title. The peasants were trying to get him to eat pork, to do every-thing that was against his beliefs. She noticed how excited I was getting, sitting up in the bed, and she asked me what was so good about it. So I read her a bit. About a party up in the mountains. Poland, this was, four hundred years ago. Jacob was sent up there in the summer months to look after the cattle, find them grass among the rocks, and the only other people there with him were the village freaks, the products of brothers riding the sisters and the rest of it. Granted, the writer expressed it a bit better than I can, but you get my drift. So I read her a bit. I can't quote it exactly but they were all rolling around in the muck, grunting like pigs, barking like dogs, howling, pissing on the fire, hugging the trees, stretched out on the rocks, vomiting, screaming, roaring.

—It's just like our wedding, she said.—What's it about besides that bit?

—Well, it's a love story, I said.—It's fantastic.

—Find us a different bit, she said.

So I did. Where he describes Wanda, this peasant girl that Jacob loves. And that's when it happened. I got through a page and a half, which wasn't too bad because it was very small print and long paragraphs. Anyway, I came and she collapsed on me.

—Ah look it, I said.—I've lost me page.

She laughed and cried, you know the way, and kissed me.

—That's the one, she said, into my ear.

Meaning, she'd be pregnant. She took the book out from between us and looked at the cover, at the writer's name.

—We'll call him Isaac, if it's a boy, she said.

It wasn't anything, actually. Not that time. But that's how important it was to me, reading, music, even the job. I *loved* tiles. Holding them, lining them up. The word 'grout'. Everything.

She gave me the job of naming the kids. She knew I'd give them names that meant something. That had a bit of magic in them. So the eldest is Sarah. That's the name Wanda changed her name to after she ran off with Jacob, in *The Slave*. She read the book last year, the eldest did, and I think she was pleased, even though it's very sad in places and Sarah has a hard time of it. She said nothing, but I think she liked it, the link there, you know. Then there's Oskar, from *The Tin Drum*. She wasn't too keen on him being named after a dwarf but I persuaded her that if our lad got up to half the things that Oskar does in the book then we'd never be bored. Then there's Mary, from *Strumpet City*. She's a great fighter, Mary in that book. And we thought we'd go for something a bit more Irish, even though it's not strictly an Irish name. But, anyway, she's Mary. And the little lad is Chili, after Chili Palmer in *Get Shorty*. He's actually named after me, Terence, because we knew he'd more than likely be the last and she said we should name him after me and my father. I didn't mind. I quite liked it, actually. Even though I've been reading books all my life and I've never come across a hero or even a baddie called Terence. But, anyway, we usually call him Chili. And that's Chili in the book, not John Travolta in the film, good and all as he was.

Anyway, the point is, I haven't always been the miserable poor shite you're looking at. And, really, it wasn't too bad until recently. I'm just so tired, you know. And then this thing.

How it happened was, we got up together one Saturday morning and found the kitchen flooded. Water all over the shop. But we couldn't see where it was coming from. I turned it off at the mains and we found it, the source of the leak. There's a rubber pipe that runs from the cold tap to a tap outside on the wall. A mouse had eaten into it. The plumber, a pal of mine, showed it to us when he was replacing it. The teeth marks.

—These things are supposed to be rodent-proof, he says.

—Tell that to the fuckin' mouse, she says.

And that was that, really. No real damage done. I got some poison, the blue stuff – I can't remember its name – and I put it up in the attic. And I got a couple of new traps for in here. No problem, end of story. Then I found your man and we realised that it was a rat all the time and he'd had the run of the house for God knows how long.

So. I suppose, on top of everything else, my tiredness, the rows with the eldest – I suppose I'm just getting old. The rat was the icing on the cake, so to speak. Not the first time I've seen a rat, of course. I see them all the time on the job, and when I was a kid we used to hunt them. But before, when I saw a rat, it was always doing the decent thing, running off in the opposite direction. This guy, though. Granted, he was dead. But how long had he been in the house? Mice stick to one little patch of the house, but not rats. They have the run of the place. He came into the kitchen here through a hole in the plaster, where it was drenched by the flooding and fell away from the wall. He died two feet from the hole. But what about before that? How did he get in before the plaster fell away? Down the stairs? It's shattering, thinking about it.

But.

Here it is. Here's why I'm here. I'm taking the house back. I'm repossessing it. I'm staying here like this until it becomes natural again. Until I'm actually reading, and not listening out for noise or remembering our dead pal on the floor every time I go over to the kettle.

I'm not guarding the house. I don't think that there are more rats inside. Or mice. And, to be honest with you, the mice are fuckin' welcome. I'll get in some extra cheese for them. No, I'm getting over that bit. That's only a matter of time. The rat's gone.

But. In a way, I *am* guarding the house. Not against a rat or rats or anything else that shouldn't be in the house. I'm guarding it against nature. The only reason life can go on in this house is because we managed to keep nature out. And it's the same with every house. And nature isn't lambs and bunnies and David Attenborough – that's only a tiny part of it. It's a lot rougher than that. Life is a fight between us – the humans, like – and nature. We've been winning but we haven't won. And we never will. The rats, for instance. They're under us. Three feet, about. A bit more, a bit less. They're under there. Fine. But give them a chance and they'll be back. They haven't lost and they never will. We need the walls and the foundations to keep them out, to let them know – because they're not thick – we're brighter than them and we're stronger than them. We have to mark off our space, the same as the other animals do.

And it's not just the animals. It's ourselves. We used to be cannibals. It's only natural, when you think about it. We're only meat. What could be more natural, for fuck sake? We probably taste quite good as well, the fitter, younger ones. But we sorted out the cannibalism years ago. It's not an issue any more, it's not a choice. Take the house away, though, take the farms and the roads and all the organisation that goes into human life and it will be a question of choice again. If nature gets the upper hand again, we'll soon be eating each other. Or, at the very least, we'll be deciding whether or not to. And then there's sex. We're only a couple of generations away from the poor freaks in *The Slave*. Brothers with sisters, fathers with daughters. It goes on anyway, sometimes. We all know that. It's disgusting, but we have to admit it. It's nothing new. I've always known it. Only, I've never had to think about it. And that's what the rat did when it decided to die on the floor over there.

I recognise what's going on in my head, what's been going on for a while, actually, on and off. It's middle age. I know that. It's getting older, slower, tired, bored, useless. It's death becoming something real. The old neighbours from my childhood dying. And even people my own age. Cancer, mostly.

But you can still hang on. And I'd been doing alright. There's little Chili. He's been like a new battery. Just picking him up strips the years off me. I feel as young and as happy as I did when Sarah was born. And there's Jackie. We get on great. We have sex, although it always seems to be on Fridays. Which I don't like, that kind of routine. Because I'm a bastard for routines. The slightest excuse, everything becomes a routine, and I've always tried to fight it. But anyway. I love her. Yeah, I do.

She makes me laugh. She knows I'm struggling, and she's sympathetic. She gets a bit impatient with me, but who wouldn't be.

I'd been coping okay. Enjoying life. The world was a straightforward, decent place that could be simplified into a line of words running down a blackboard. My very educated mother just showed us nine planets.

And so it is. Only, it has to be protected. If you find a rat in your kitchen the world stops being a straight-forward, decent place for a while. You have to take it back. And that's what I'm doing. Taking it back.

And I'm getting there. I don't know how long it's going to take, and I don't care. Fuck the rat. And fuck nature.

It's a matter of time.

The Joke

If he went now, he'd never come back. He'd go and she wouldn't know, or care. He'd come back and the same thing; she wouldn't care. So, what was the point? He wasn't going anywhere.

And that made it worse. And made him more annoyed. And angry. And stupid.

This thing now. It was nothing. The thing itself.

—No, no. He'll come and collect you.

That was it. Word for word. What had him half standing, still sitting, his fat arse hanging over the armchair.

His arse wasn't fat. But there was more of it than there used to be. Not that much more.

Anyway.

They were the words.

—No, no. He'll come and collect you.

The words themselves were harmless. She hadn't even been talking to him.

But that, there, was the point. She hadn't been talking to him. She'd been talking to someone else. She still was.

On the phone. He didn't know who. Her sister, her ma, his ma. They were the even-money bets. But it could have been anyone. Her friend, the adultery woman, was another prospect. She was a three-to-one bet.

He wasn't a betting man. Never had been.

She was out in the kitchen; he didn't know who she was talking to. But he did know that she'd just offered his services to whoever it was at the other end.

—No, no. He'll come and collect you.

And that was the thing. And had been the thing for a long time. And he was sick of it.

Sick of what, but?

He wasn't sure. The whole thing. Everything. He was just sick of it.

The invisible fuckin' man.

—No, no. He'll come and collect you.

That was who he was. What he was. The invisible man. The taken-for-granted sap. As if he was just waiting there. With nothing better to do.

Granted, he was doing nothing. But that wasn't the point. No way was it. He'd been sitting there, doing nothing in particular – the telly was off. But it didn't matter. If he'd been climbing Mount Everest or upstairs in the bed, it didn't matter. It didn't bloody matter what he was or wasn't doing.

It was the fact, the thing. He didn't know how to—

Just hearing it. He was sick of it. And he couldn't say anything. Because it was so small. He could never explain it without being mean or selfish or other things that he really wasn't.

Her friend, for example. The adultery woman. They'd been friends for years. A good-looking woman. Didn't nearly look her age. And the adultery thing wasn't fair. He wasn't judging. He didn't; he never had.

Anyway. He'd been there when she'd left her husband. He'd helped her load the car, *his* car, with her bags and her two kids and all of their stuff. While the husband was at work, or wherever – the pub; he didn't know. And he was glad he'd done it. It had been the right thing to do. He'd never doubted it. Not once. Or resented it, or anything. The husband was a bollix, an animal. She was well out of that situation. And he wouldn't have cared if the husband had come after him. The woman's jaw was strapped and broken, sitting beside him in the car. The kids in the back were pale. It had been a good deed, that one. He'd felt a bit heroic. The wife had hugged him, kissed him, thanked him again and again.

That was the biggest example. The most dramatic.

He wasn't making his point. He was missing it.

A better example. Her mother. Not such a bad oul' one. Harmless really, once you knew her. Anyway, he'd gone out in the pissing rain to bring her home from her bingo. More than once, and no problem. He'd been happy to do it; he'd do it again. And her sister. He'd brought her twenty Silk Cut when she was stuck at home with her broken leg. And a choc-ice.

Errands of mercy. He'd been doing them for years. And here – good – here was the point. Not once, not once – none of them had ever asked him.

She was still on the phone.

—Yeah, I know, yeah. God.

Not once. Fair enough, they'd all said thanks.

You're great.

You're a star.

I don't know where I'd be without you.

And that was fine. And appreciated. But none of them had ever phoned and asked to speak to him. Not once. Ever.

And it wasn't just that.

It was—

Fuckin' everything. He was sick of it.

But he sat down again. His arms were getting sore, holding himself over the seat. But that didn't mean anything. He hadn't changed his mind; he hadn't made it up. He could get back up; he would. She was still on the phone. It wasn't urgent, whatever it was. He had to clear his head. He had to be clear. He was going to say no when she came looking for him. He had to know why.

It went back. Back, back, back. Ah, Jesus – years. His fault. He accepted that. Yeah. His own fault. So.

But it wasn't about the errands of mercy. She'd called them that. It wasn't just them. He had to be clear.

He'd liked it; he remembered. When she'd said that about errands of mercy. She was drying his hair with a towel. She sat on his lap. One leg each side of his legs, right up at him.

He still had his hair. Most of it.

Lap was a stupid word.

He loved her. That was important.

Back.

Give and take. There'd once been that. Partnership. That was what he'd have called it, although he didn't like that word either. Partnership. Give and take. He brought her ma home from bingo; she sat on his lap. But that wasn't it; that just cheapened it. It wasn't about the sex. But—

That too. Yeah, definitely.

How, but –? How was he going to get his point across without making it look like it was all about sex when it wasn't but, in a way, it was?

He'd deal with it.

Anyway.

Partnership. It had all been part of it. The relationship – another fuckin' word. They'd done things together. Even when they weren't together. He'd do the driving or the shop, clean the windows, whatever. But they'd both be involved. They'd done them together. That was how it had felt. How it had been.

Something had happened.

Nothing had happened. It had just happened. The way things were now.

She was still in there, on the phone. He could hear her agreeing and disagreeing, with whoever. Listening, nodding. Putting her hair behind her ear.

He still loved her.

And the partnership had stopped. Somewhere. He could never have pinned it down; he'd no idea. There'd been nothing said. Nothing done. As far as he knew. But, who knew?

71

It was a mess. He was. A mess. His anger. Moods.

He wanted to reach out. In the bed. And he couldn't. It wasn't there; he couldn't do it. He couldn't lift his hand and move it, a foot, a foot and a half – less. He couldn't do it. What had happened? What had happened?

He didn't know. He honestly didn't. He didn't know.

It was a good big telly, one of the widescreen ones. He'd thought they could watch it together. At least that. When he'd bought it.

He was older. Fuck that, so was she. That wasn't it. He didn't think it was.

They'd never spoken about it.

What?

He didn't know. The change. The stop. He didn't know. The partnership. Fuck it, the marriage. And it wasn't true about the sex either, exactly. They still had it, did it. Now and again. The odd time. The hands would meet. The warmth.

What was he going to say? When she came in?

She was still in there, in the kitchen. Still chatting.

He was right but. Essentially, he was right. It was gone. Something had gone wrong. Something small. Something that he hadn't even noticed. It had changed. She couldn't deny it.

And would she? Deny it. He hadn't a clue.

He used to know. He used to guess right, more often than not. What she'd say. How she'd react. They'd smile at each other, because they both knew what they were up to. She'd slap his arse when he passed. He'd put his hand on her hair. Words hadn't mattered; she'd known what he meant. I love you. I like you. I'm glad.

I love you. I like you. I'm glad.

That was it.

He used to – he could tell when she was going to say something. Before she did. Something in the air, in the atmosphere. He didn't have to be looking at her. He knew. And she did too. And he'd liked being read.

He didn't know when it had stopped. The reading. He didn't know. Maybe they still could, read each other's thoughts; they just didn't. He didn't know; he didn't think so. He didn't know her. He *knew* her, but he didn't know her. It had been a slow thing. Very gradual. He hadn't noticed.

That wasn't true. He had. He'd noticed.

But he'd done nothing.

What?

Jesus, it was terrible. Stupid.

He was angry. He was always angry.

He was always angry.

He lay awake, he woke early. It was always there. He didn't know why. Nothing had happened. Nothing big. His fault. He should have known. It was there a long time, the difference. The silence. He'd known.

They'd never had a row. That was true, more or less. There'd never been anything serious. Small stuff. Missing keys, her ma at Christmas. Nothing big. Fundamental. Neither of them had ever stormed out or packed a bag. They'd never shouted or broken anything. There'd been nothing like that. There'd been nothing.

Maybe it was the kids.

He was blaming the kids.

He wasn't. Just, maybe that was part of what had happened. They'd never had time; they'd been too busy. Always ferrying them around, football and dancing and Scouts and discos. Then ferrying her ma as well. And her sister, and his ma. And her friend. The one he'd driven away from her husband.

He'd had a thing about her. He'd have admitted that. It had never come to anything. But he'd felt it. A woman who'd had sex with someone she wasn't married to. He'd been excited. That was true. At the time. Even with her kids in the back of the car. Adultery. Another word that did nothing for him.

The kids but. There was nothing in that theory. They'd been busy, run off their feet – mad stuff. But they'd had the kids in common. Even when they were upstairs, in the bed.

Is that one of them waking?

Don't stop, don't stop.

Where's his inhaler?

Don't stop!

They'd liked it. They'd loved it. At the time. And it had been a long time. Twenty-six years. What had happened?

He didn't fuckin' know.

Did she?

He didn't know.

Probably.

He didn't know.

He didn't know anything.

The telly hadn't worked. Not really. Stupid, again. The idea that a television could bring them together. Even a good one. They didn't even watch telly much. They never had. He liked the football, now and again; he wasn't that fussed. She liked the politics. *Questions and Answers*. *Prime Time*. There was another telly, upstairs in the bedroom. You didn't need a big screen to watch politicians. The whole idea had been stupid.

The football was better on the big screen but.

He felt himself smiling. Like a fight against his face. He let it through. He smiled.

She was still on the phone. She laughed.

Like the old times. He'd smiled; she'd laughed. The way they used to know each other.

Stupid.

He was being stupid. It wasn't like the old times, nothing like the old times – whatever they were. He was by himself. She was somewhere else. There was no togetherness in it. None.

It was nice but. Her laugh. He'd always liked it.

He used to make her laugh.

God.

Could he still? Make her laugh. He doubted it. Would she want him to? He didn't know.

But he'd done it before. He'd tickled her, now and again. He couldn't do that now. Creep up behind her in the bathroom. They were never in the bathroom together. He smiled again. The thought. Creeping up behind her. She'd have fuckin' freaked. And it wasn't the only way he'd made her laugh. Words used to do it. Jokes. Play-acting, acting the eejit. She'd liked it. She'd loved it. She'd moved closer to him when she was laughing.

He could give it a try. Now. A joke. Paddy the Englishman and Paddy the Irishman were—. No; it was stupid. There was the one about the guy with no back passage. No. The one about the Irishman at the Tina Turner concert. He smiled. Too long, and she hadn't liked it the first time. He remembered.

What was he doing?

He wasn't sure.

What's the difference between a good ride and a good shite? That was a good one. Short and good. But it was so long since he'd told her a joke. He was just being thick.

They hadn't spoken since this morning.

There's the rain now.

Yeah.

There's the rain now. Him.

Yeah. Her.

And that was nearly – he looked at his watch – eight hours ago. And now he wanted to tell her a joke. It was mad. What's the difference between a good ride and a good shite?

Mad.

Thick. Stupid.

He wasn't angry now but. He wasn't sure why he'd been angry.

That wasn't true. He knew. But he wasn't angry now.

He'd tell her the joke. He was nervous now. It was a

76

good one to tell but. It was short, no story to it. He'd see if it worked as he told it.

What would he see? He didn't know. It was what he wanted to see; that was the thing. Her face. He wanted to see her listening – that was all. See her face, see her listening. Knowing what he was up to. That would do.

He listened. She was out there, in the kitchen. He could hear her shoes. He knew, somehow – he didn't know how: she was finishing up. The way she was moving, like she was leaving. She was going to hang up.

What's the difference between a good ride and a good shite? He couldn't do it. It was too mad, too desperate. She'd recognise it for what it was: begging. A cry for fuckin' help.

That was stupid too but. It wasn't a cry for anything. And it wasn't fuckin' begging. It was only a joke. There it was now; she'd put the phone down. She was still in the kitchen. It was more than a joke. He knew that.

Would she know?

He could hear her now.

She came to the door. She stopped.

He looked at her.

Ash

—We'll still be friends, she said.

    —Grand, he answered, and then he was walking down a street by himself, before he fully understood what had happened. He knew the street, although not very well. He wasn't sure why he was there, why they'd gone over to this part of the city. His wife had just told him she was leaving him. Or he was leaving her. One or the other.

And they'd still be friends.

Grand.

He made it home. He got the Dart, figured out how to get a one-way ticket out of the vending machine at the station. He'd left the car for his wife. She wasn't there when he got in. He paid the babysitter.

Later, Ciara came home. And she was all over him. She climbed onto him and cried as she came.

—I'm so, so sorry.

And that was that, he thought, if it had ever been anything in the first place. He didn't want to ask her if she'd actually told him that she was leaving him. He knew she had. It didn't matter.

—You'll be fine, she said, after she'd kissed his stomach and lay tucked in beside him. He'd passed a test, or something. He was delighted. She was gone in the morning.

He went to work. The house was empty when he got home after collecting the girls. He thought: *This is it, this is me. I live alone. With the kids.* She'd taken nothing. The bedroom was exactly the same. Her book was still beside the bed.

She came in very late. He wasn't sure – he didn't know – if she'd changed her mind or if she'd just come home later than usual. She was drunk – he didn't ask. She rode him again, said nothing about being sorry this time. She didn't cry.

Then she was gone again.

He put Erica and Wanda to bed again the next night, made them brush their teeth, read a story to them. *Kipper's Toybox*, twice.

—Where's Mammy?

—Work.

—Poor Mammy.

—Yeah.

He turned off their light and made sure their bedroom door was open exactly as wide as they wanted it.

—More.

—No, stop.

—More.

He went downstairs. Ciara didn't come in. He put the mobile phone beside him, on the arm of the chair.

He watched telly. He slept. She didn't phone. He went up to the bed. He turned off the light.

He woke up. She wasn't there. Three in the morning. And she wasn't downstairs. He went back up to the bed but he didn't sleep. He went down to the kitchen again. He accepted it as he put the coffee on the hob: *She's left me*.

—You think she has? said his brother, Mick.

—Yeah.

They were in the kitchen.

—You *think*? said Mick.

—Yeah.

—Well, like. Did she actually tell you she was leaving?

—Yeah, he said.—I think so.

—You fuckin' think so? Jesus, Kev, you can fuckin' do better than that.

—She told me.

—Grand. And what happened then?

—She rode the arse off me.

—Strange, said Mick.—But it makes sense too. The long goodbye. The ride of the guilty. You've heard of it.

—No.

—It's brilliant, said Mick.—I recommend it. What happened then?

—I think she went to work.

—Is she riding anyone else?

The question shocked him. Although it shouldn't have. It annoyed him, the invasion. And frightened him.

—I don't think so, he said.

—Think again.

—As far as I know.

—Okay.

—How would I know?

—Well, said Mick. —She might have told you.

—No.

—Sure?

—Yeah. I think so – no – yeah.

—Okay, said Mick.—Credit card statements.

—Hang on, said Kevin.—It's the man who always gets caught because of his credit card. Am I right?

Mick shrugged.

—Does she have her own card?

—Yeah, said Kevin. —'Course.

—So, let's have a gawk. It can do no harm.

Kevin was starting to dislike his brother, but this wasn't a new feeling.

—No, he said.

Mick shrugged again. He was a cunt for the shrugging.

—Okay, he said.

He stood up. He had to go to their mother's.

—She's complaining about the jacks.

—She's always complaining.

—Ah, she's not the worst, said Mick.—It won't turn off properly, or something.

—The toilet?

—Yeah, said Mick.—She says it sounds like the cistern is talking to her when she's downstairs and it's upstairs.

—It's always upstairs. It's attached to the fuckin' wall.

—You're becoming a very bitter little man, Kev.

—Fuck off, Mick.

—This is me fucking off, said Mick as he walked to the back door.—Away, to have a chat with our mother's toilet. What a fuckin' life. Good luck.

Kevin took out the accordion file where they kept the bank statements, the insurance stuff, birth certificates, and all the other crap they were supposed to keep. It was in the wardrobe, at the back, behind her shoes and boots, a heap of the things.

He sat on the bed and held one of her high heels as he looked at a recent statement. He put the page on a pillow, propped a bit, and he read it from a distance. He didn't really read it – you couldn't read a bank statement. He gave it a quick look; he glanced down the page.

—Why are you holding Mammy's shoe?

It was Erica, the younger one.

—What makes you think it's Mammy's shoe?

He hadn't a clue why he'd said that.

—It is, said Erica.

—You're right, said Kevin.—It was on the floor. Do you want to put it back?

—Can I, like, wear them?

—Yeah, alright.

—Can Wanda?

—Yeah.

—Wanda!

He left the girls in the bedroom lining up the shoes.

—Where's Mammy?

—Work.

—Poor Mammy.

—That's right.

—Always working.

—Now you're talking.

He went downstairs.

—Nothing, he said, when Mick answered his mobile.

—What?

—I looked. There's nothing on the credit card statement.

—Nothing incriminating, no?

—Jesus, Mick, take it easy.

—Well, said Mick.—What were you looking for?

—I don't know, said Kevin.

He was regretting he'd called Mick now. Big time. But he'd had to.

—A name or something, he said.

—A name? said Mick.—What name? D'you think she's paying whoever she's having the affair with?

—No. What affair?

—Or it's a rent boy or something. She has to pay someone to—

—No. Fuck off.

—Any restaurants?

—No.

—Hotels?

—No.

—He's paying, so.

—Who?

—The rent boy.

—Fuck off, Mick.

—Stranger things have happened, man. People go off the rails in times of recession. Especially women.

—What are you on about?

—The moral compass, man, said Mick.—They try to ride the fuckin' thing.

—Goodnight.

Mick texted him.

Hav u foned hr?

No.

Wy not?

He phoned Mick.

—Because I'm frightened.

—Okay, said Mick.—I'm with you.

Mick wasn't the worst, Kevin thought.

—What would you do? he asked.

—Well look it, man, said Mick.—Just to remind you. I live in a poxy one-room flat because I had a short, meaningless fling with my son's religion and civics teacher, who gave him a note to give to me and he – and I love my son, I blame only myself – he gave the note to his mother instead. Who read it, and it said—

—I know.

—You can do it to me that way next time.

—I know, sorry.

—Ten words that shook the fuckin' world.

They were enjoying themselves.

—And you want to know what I'd do if I was in your position?

—Yeah, said Kevin.—I do.

—Grand, said Mick.—I haven't a clue.

—Goodnight, Mick.

—Go a bit mad.

—Thanks.

—You asked.

—How?

—How what?

—How would I go mad?

—Wife-swapping.

—I'd need a wife.

—True.

—Goodnight, Mick.

—Let me work on it.

—Goodnight.

—I'll get back to you.

—Okay.

He went to his room – their room – and started throwing the shoes back into the wardrobe.

—Excuse me!

It was Erica.

—We're, like, trying to sleep in here!

—Yeah!

—Sorry.

He got down on his knees and put the shoes and boots away, quietly. He piled them. The wardrobe door swung slowly towards him and with it the full-length mirror.

He looked, and saw nothing. He wasn't there. He pushed the door back slightly. And there he was.

He got into bed. He phoned her. Her voicemail was gone. It was the automated voice, the Vodafone woman, telling him to leave a message. He had nothing ready and he couldn't think of anything he wanted to say out loud – *the kids miss you; I miss you; where the fuck are you, you stupid mad bitch of a cunt?* – so he said nothing.

Mick texted.

Jaksns, snday.

Jackson's was a pub near Mick's place. It was an ordinary pub six nights a week but on Sundays, according to Mick, it changed. It filled up with men – *in wmn* – of a certain age, who were no longer married or had never been married.

—People like you.

—Exactly, said Mick.

—And that's going wild, is it? said Kevin.—Going to a pub full of Micks?

They were laughing.

—Works for me, said Mick.—No one goes home empty-handed.

—Lovely, said Kevin.—I can't wait.

—I'm telling yeh, man, said Kevin.—I went home the last time with fifty-seven-year-old twins.

—Oh Jesus.

—Combined age, one hundred and fourteen.

—Goodnight, Mick.

—Next Sunday, so.

—No, fuck off. I'll think about it.

—Do that.

—Goodnight.

He did think about it. Sunday was four days away. He'd need a babysitter. The young one from next door. Grace. The girls loved her. He could only stay out till eleven, because Grace would have school on Monday. That would give him two hours in Jackson's. Two hours of abandonment. Then he'd have to come home. He'd come into the house and pay Grace, while Mick's twins hid behind the car till the coast was clear. Or he could sneak them up the stairs, then go back down to pay Grace and send her home. Or he'd sneak them up the stairs – they'd be pissed and too skinny and giggling – into the bedroom, and Ciara would be in the bed, waiting for him. He'd sneak them up the stairs, send Grace home, then stand at the bottom of the stairs, all night, till he could go to work. He'd sneak them up the stairs, and – he could see this now; he groaned – they'd go into the wrong room and wake Erica and Wanda. *Oops!* Or, he'd go to Jackson's, have three pints, and come home. Mad.

Wild.

It wasn't funny.

He'd stop at the chipper on the way home.

It wasn't funny.

He wasn't going anywhere on Sunday. Mick and his fuckin' twins.

He woke before Ciara got into the bed.

—Hi, she said.

—Hi.

—I don't want to have sex with you.

—Fine.

She climbed in. He didn't have to move. He was lying on his side of the bed. She lay back, and turned. She put her hand on his shoulder. She patted it – he thought she did. He felt her breath. He could smell it. No wine or anything – just toothpaste. He was asleep before her – he thought he was. And she was there when he woke.

She came into the kitchen. The girls were still asleep. *They'll be delighted to see you.* It was business as usual, although they managed to avoid touching or looking at one another. *So are you back, or what?* She cleared the old plates off the table. She got a cloth from the sink, wiped the table and put four bowls and four spoons on the place mats.

—We'll have to talk, she said.

He chopped a banana, to put on top of the girls' cornflakes.

—Okay, he said.

About what?

He threw the banana's brown skin in the bin, so the girls wouldn't see it and object. He looked, but Ciara wasn't in the kitchen.

She'd gone up to wake the girls. He could hear the squeals. He didn't want to hear them laughing; she didn't deserve them – he didn't want to think that. He turned on the radio, to get the news. He was bang-on, half-seven. He actually listened.

He ran to the hall.

—Come down, quick!

88

—Why?

—The news! Come on!

They all sat in front of the telly and watched the Icelandic volcano erupting.

—Amazing.

They looked at the cloud as it grew and curled.

—It's all ash, he told them.

—What's ash?

Erica's question – it was one of those brilliant moments. Kevin and Ciara looked at each other. They smiled. There were no coal fires in the house and neither of them had ever smoked. The cooker was electric. Nothing was ever burned. There was no real religion, at home or in school, so Erica had never noticed the grey thumbprints on Ash Wednesday, on the foreheads of the old and the Polish. A child like Erica could get this far without knowing what ash was, until she saw it spewing from a mountain.

—It's like dust, he said.—Burnt.

—What burnt?

—Stone, I think. I'm not sure.

—Stone?

—I think so.

—You, like, can't burn stone.

—If it's hot enough, you can. Lava.

—It's scary.

—It's only a cloud.

They sat and watched, and ate, and gathered the expertise. Ash killed planes; it attached itself to the turbine section of the engines.

It was an act of God.

—What's that?

—Nature.

It had nothing to do with climate change or the economy. No one was to blame. All flights in and out of Ireland, in and out of Europe and everywhere, were cancelled. The airports were crowded and shut. There was no escape.

—Does that mean there'll never be any more planes?

—No, said Kevin.—It doesn't.

He looked at Ciara.

—It's just for a while. Things will get back to normal after the ash drifts away. Or falls.

—Falls?

—Yeah.

—Will it hurt?

—No, said Ciara.—It won't.

Funerals

His parents went to the chipper after funerals. Bill found this out when he drove them home from one – the dead husband of his mother's long-dead sister. He'd driven them there because the church and the graveyard were down the country, in a small kip of a village that seemed untouched by the now dead boom, except for the fact that the priest was Polish. His father wasn't happy driving off the main roads any more, and his mother had shrunk. She couldn't reach the pedals.

So she said.

Bill had said he'd bring them, and they'd climbed into the back of the car like they were his kids and they were all going off on a picnic. Already, he was making it up. He couldn't wait to tell his wife and kids – his real kids.

He even bought them ice creams on the way.

He didn't actually do that, but it was what he told

Hazel and the girls when he got home. He saw the big cone outside a shop ahead of them.

—D'yis fancy a 99?

—Ah, no, said his mother.—It wouldn't be right.

—Go on. Where's the harm?

—Alright.

He had them licking away in the back of the car while he turned off the main road, onto a glorified lane that was all corners and gear changes.

They found the village. He drove through it before he knew they were there.

There was the mass. The priest sounded like a culchie who'd spent his childhood in Eastern Europe.

—Paddy was populler wit' al' the neighbours.

—He was not, he heard his father whisper.

—Shush, Liam.

There was the walk to the graveyard.

—There's the clouds now, look.

—We'll be drenched before he's buried.

—We might make it.

—Wait and see. The bastard's up there, orchestrating the whole thing.

The coffin was lowered and they went back to the village's one pub for coffee and a few sandwiches. Bill met cousins he didn't know he had and an uncle he thought had died in 1994. He kissed a woman's cheek because he thought they were related, then watched her filling a tray with empty cups and bringing it through a door behind the counter.

They went back to the car. His father climbed

into the front this time. Bill turned the car towards Dublin.

—All this fresh air, said his father.—It's not good for a man.

—I was surprised there were so many there, said his mother, in the back. —He was a cranky enough little man.

—It's a small town, said his father. —A village. They'd have to go.

—I wouldn't have gone.

—You were there.

—That's different, said his mother.—He was my sister's husband.

His father turned – groaned – so he could look at Bill.

—That was how I ended up with your mother, he said.—Her sister dumped me for the bollix we just buried.

—Don't listen to him, said his mother; she was laughing.

—A fine bit of stuff she was too, said his father.

—Ah now, said his mother.—She had nothing on me.

—She had morals, though, said his father.

—Ah, Liam!

Bill could laugh. He could enjoy their company and listen to them flirting. They weren't his parents any more; he wasn't their son. He was a middle-aged man in a car with two people who were a bit older. Once or twice, in a rush that made him hang onto the steering wheel, he *was* their son and the car was full of himself as a boy and a stupid, awkward young man, hundreds of boys and men, all balled into this one man driving his wife's Toyota Corolla and trying not to cry.

He drove back up to the main road, straight past the big ice-cream cone.

—There's a tractor in the field there, look.

—That's the place for tractors.

His father's sarcasm, his mother setting him up, the easy words they'd always petted one another with, even when they were angry, the routine Bill had loved, then hated and hated and hated, until he'd started to hear it in his own kitchen and he saw his daughter – she was twenty-two now – strapped into her high chair, looking from him to her mother, back to him, her big eyes like spotlights following them.

He slowed down, indicated right. They were home, at the corner of the cul-de-sac, a hundred yards from the house he'd grown up in.

—No no, said his father.—Go on ahead. You can drop us off at the chipper.

—The chipper?

His mother, behind him, explained.

—We always go to the chipper after a funeral.

—That's right, said his father, and Bill could hear him shifting in the seat so he could look at Bill full on.

—Grand, said Bill.

He looked in the rear-view, made sure there was nothing behind them, and kept going, to the row of shops, Costcutter's, Ladbrokes, the chemist, the chipper.

None of them had been there when Bill was a kid. The chipper had been a hardware shop.

—Mind you, love, said his father, to his mother.—The amount of funerals we're going to, we might have to pick and choose.

He patted his stomach. He actually thumped it.

—We can't be eating chips every day.

—I don't know, said his mother.—I have the waist I had when I was ten.

She was probably telling the truth.

There was a space outside the chipper. Bill took it. He looked over his shoulder, at his mother.

—There y'are, Miss Daisy.

—You're a better-looking man than Morgan Freeman, she said.

—Who's Morgan Freeman?

—An actor, said Bill.

—Black, said his mother.—He's very good.

—What was he in?

—Lots of things.

They hadn't moved to get out of the car. There was a queue inside the chipper, five or six people.

—Do you bring the chips home? he asked.

He was hoping they wouldn't expect him to wait.

—Usually, yes, said his mother.

—But not today, said his father.—There's another funeral on the agenda.

The ex-President, Paddy Hillery, had died. His hearse would be going past the top of the road, on its way to the graveyard in Sutton.

—We're going to go up and watch, said his father.

He opened his door. Bill heard him groan as he got one leg out and leaned forward.

—That rain's staying away.

Bill got out and opened the door for his mother. She looked so small, just a little head and a coat. He'd never get used to being much taller than her.

He kissed her cheek.

—Enjoy the funeral.

—Paddy Hillery was a decent man, she said. —Not like the crowd that are there today.

—You're right there. Seeyeh, Da.

—Good luck.

He got back into the car, reversed slowly, and watched them walk, slowly, into the chipper, to the back of the queue. His father stood aside to let her go in first. She was taking her purse from her coat pocket. He decided not to hit the horn. He went on to work.

In the version he told the family later, he watched the funeral with them. He added the chips to the 99s. He planted himself beside them, the three of them sitting on a wall – he had to lift his mother – as they watched the ex-President's hearse go by, and the limos with the widow and family and the country's leaders.

—Here's poor Paddy now.

Politicians had always been known by their first names, even nicknames. But that had stopped. It was surnames only now.

—He wasn't the worst.

—He had a bit of dignity about him.

—That's it, said his father.—Over. These cars here are just caught behind the funeral.

—We'll go home, so, and watch it on the telly.

Bill didn't know why he did it, why he embellished, or just made up, his parents' lives. They didn't need it.

But he did.

He started going to more funerals with them. The ones that needed a bit of travel. He'd drive them there and home. Men his father had worked with, or their wives, even their children. Cousins of his mother's. Old friends, women his mother had gone to school with. They'd make a day of it, stop for coffee, look at a monument. He stayed clear of the local funerals, the old neighbours. He didn't want the conversations. *What are you up to these days? How many kids is it you have?* He didn't want to talk to men he'd once known who'd lost their jobs so recently they still didn't understand it. *Great, great. Yourself?* There'd be too many middle-aged women who used to be girls, ponytailed men he used to play with, a mother he'd fancied – in the coffin. Fat grannies he'd kissed and – the last time he'd gone to one of the local ones – a woman with MS, shaking her way to a seat in the church, the first girl he'd ever had sex with.

And there were the Alzheimer's stories. The parents of friends he'd grown up with. He'd listen to their children while they waited outside the church for the hearse and told him about the Saturday mornings or Sunday afternoons, the drive to nursing homes out past the edge of Dublin, sitting with the women or men who'd reared them – who'd helped rear Bill – who hadn't a clue who their children were. There was the angry, roaring woman who'd been lovely, and the man – he'd trained Bill's under-15s Gaelic team – who claimed he'd piloted his plane into both Twin Towers. There was the eighty-seven-year-old grandmother who'd slept her way to the top. *The top of what? She never says. She just likes saying 'Fucked'. She never fuckin' blinks.* And the man who'd gone to school with Robert Mugabe. *They were all bright sparks, the Mugabes.* The stories, the laughter, followed quickly by the violence, stenches, stares into nothing, silence. *Jesus, Billy, you're lucky.*

He phoned his parents every Sunday night. His father always answered and immediately got rid of the phone because his hearing aid was roaring.

—I'll hand you over to your mother!

He'd hear her walking across the room to take the cordless phone from his father.

—Hello?

—Howyeh.

—Ah, William. How's everyone?

She'd tell him if he was needed for the first half of the week.

—Nothing to report. No one's dead since the last time.

He'd feel relieved, and let down. The fact was, his own job was crumbling away. There was still work – there always would be – but less of it, and less. He sold insurance, group policies, to companies, nearly all of them small, even during the boom years. SMEs, as he'd learnt to call them. Small and medium enterprises. He'd noticed it about eighteen months before: he was frightened whenever he phoned one of the men or women he'd done happy business with for years, hoping they'd answer, hoping they wouldn't. He'd put it off. He'd drive past, see if the place was still open, then park and phone. The funerals filled his week.

But there was more to it. Maybe it was his age, maybe the fact that his kids weren't kids now, that they were becoming people he used to know, like the old friends at the funerals. He wanted to be with his parents. Maybe it was because they were old, no longer growing old.

He phoned again on Wednesdays.

—I'll hand you over to your mother!

—Ah, William. How's everyone?

—Grand.

—Hazel?

—Great. She says hello.

—I've a bit of news.

—Yeah?

—Martin Ferritor. He worked with your daddy, oh, years ago. When he was with Hibernian Motors.

—I don't remember him.

—Well, he's after dying, whether you remember him or not.

It was good news; they both knew it.

—Where did he live?

—Well, when your dad knew him, he lived in Whitehall.

Whitehall was ten minutes from Bill's house.

99

—But he moved to Wexford, somewhere, when he retired. Is that too far?

—No, said Bill.—I should be able to manage it. I'll need to sort a few things. When?

—Friday, she said.—I have it written down. Hang on a minute.

He heard her bringing the phone into the kitchen. He knew exactly where she was.

—Whitechapel.

She was reading the name – he could tell.

—I know Whitechapel, he told her.

—*Near* Whitechapel, she said. —You have to go through Whitechapel.

—We were there years ago. Me and Hazel. With the kids.

—Oh, that's right.

—It must be ten years, he said.—It's near Gorey.

—Oh, grand, she said.—Well, anyway, the mass is at eleven. Is it too early for you?

—I'll sort something, he said.—It'll be grand.

—Jesus, look it, said Hazel.—I don't want to be mean. But you can't bring them to every funeral, can you?

He said nothing.

—Billy?

—No.

—It's getting a little bit weird, she said.

They were out walking. If they'd been in a film, they'd have stopped and looked at one another. But it wasn't a film; they didn't stop.

—You must be going to a funeral a week, said Hazel.

She wasn't wrong. She wasn't angry either. She was still holding his arm. She wasn't pulling him back. He wasn't trying to walk away.

—It's – I don't know, he said.—I'm a bit stuck.

—How?

—Well, I did it once or twice. Drove them, you know. And it's become a bit of a routine, like. It's expected.

—It's unreasonable.

—My fault, he said. —What can I do?

—Say no.

—I do.

He had: once. But he'd driven them to five.

—Now and again is grand, said Hazel.—It's nice. But you're not a fuckin' chauffeur. You have your own life.

But it was his life, a big part of it. Going to funerals with his parents, or just being with them. He couldn't tell her. He didn't want to. They'd have stopped walking if he'd told her that. Her grip on his arm would have tightened.

—I know, he said.

Or she'd have taken her hand off his arm. She'd have stared at him.

—I can't say no this time, he said.—I've already told them I'd bring them.

—I know you enjoy it.

—I don't.

—You do, she said. —You told us. It's obvious. And it's okay. It's lovely.

101

Hazel's parents were horrible. She never went near them.

—But Jesus, she said.

—I know.

—You're busy.

—I know.

—And there's another thing, she said.—I'm jealous.

—There's no need to be.

—Well, I am. You're spending more time with them than me.

Now she stopped – kind of. She hesitated.

—And that's not natural.

She was right.

—You can come with us.

—No way, she said; she laughed.—But you can drive your own car. You're not having mine.

They were walking again. She was holding his arm. She squeezed it.

—Fair enough, he said.

His own car had needed a service, new tyres. He actually needed a new car – the lad in the garage had told him. He couldn't afford one; *they* couldn't afford one. He'd tell her soon.

His father climbed into the front seat. Every shift and push was a decision.

—Here we go again, he said.—Poor oul' Martin.

—You're the last of that gang, said his mother, in the back.

—I am, said his father.—Literally.

She was faster, nippier, like a child with arthritis. He

groaned; she didn't. The thought stung Bill: he'd be the first to go.

—The M50, said Bill.

—Grand, said his father.

They loved the new straight roads. They loved the fact that they didn't have to go through places any more.

—If we could bypass the whole bloody country we'd be sorted.

—Ah now. It's a lovely country.

—Only when you're standing on it, love.

Bill laughed. His father didn't. He groaned as he turned to look out the side window.

—Where are we now, Billy-boy?

—Past Bray, said Bill.

—Past Bray. That's great.

—Bray isn't the worst.

—That's no compliment. The worst is unbelievable.

Bill heard him turning again, adjusting himself, groaning. —Were you ever in Bundoran?

—No, said Bill.

—Don't ever go, said his father.

—I'll give it a miss.

—Do.

—I had nice Sundays in Bray, said his mother.

—It's the rest of the week I'd be worried about.

—The promenade's nice.

—Well, that's true.

—And the sea.

—The sea would be there anyway, said Bill's father.

—I knew you'd say that, said his mother.

They got to the church in plenty of time, the guts of an hour early.

—We could go have a look at Courtown.

—Then you'd lose your parking space.

They sat in the car, chatted, watched the rain spit and threaten, until more cars arrived and people got out and put on coats and jackets.

—Might as well go in.

His father was straight over to a group of people, shaking hands, laughing.

—The life and soul, said his mother. She wasn't being sarcastic.

He went with her into the church, stayed beside her on each step. The coffin was up at the front.

—God, it's dark.

—No light today at all.

They sat where they always sat, whatever church they were in, about a third of the way down, on the left side, halfway in.

—I love the smell of the polish, she whispered.

He could barely hear her. He had to lean down to get each word, to hear the full string of them. Her voice cracked on some words, whistled on others.

—The priests come and go but the women with the polish are always with us, she said.—Isn't that it?

—You're right.

—They're a disgrace.

—The women?

—The *priests*.

The hiss was louder than a shout would have been.

He was embarrassed, a child. He stopped himself from thinking: she shouldn't have opinions.

—You're right.

—Amn't I?

—Yeah.

—All those little children.

She wasn't whispering now. There weren't many in the church.

—It sickens me.

He tried to say something. He smiled at a woman three rows up who'd turned. She smiled back. A good-looking woman. Well kept. A bit heavy.

Well kept? Where had that come from? He was a child one minute, an older, much stupider man the next.

His mother was talking again.

—Your poor father.

—What?

Bill turned, to see what had happened to his father, if he'd fallen, or been drenched. But he wasn't there, at the back of the church.

—What's wrong? he asked.

—The things they did to him.

—Who?

—Are you stupid? she said.

She'd never spoken like that before, not to Bill.

—The priests!

—What about them?

She wasn't looking at him. He – now – didn't want to look at her. He thought he was going to be sick. He looked behind him again, to see if his father was there. His father would come and rescue them. But he wasn't there. Bill needed to get up, out. He'd go out and find his father.

—A terrible time they gave him, said his mother.

—Priests? said Bill.—A priest?

—Yes!

She was shouting – he thought she was. He was whispering.

—D'you want to leave? he asked.

—Why should I?

He heard feet, shoes. His father was there, making his way in, waving at someone who'd turned to look, smiling.

He sat down beside Bill.

—Here we are.

His mother leaned out a bit, so she could see past Bill.

—Is it serious out there yet?

—The rain?

—Yes.

—No, it's grand. It might stay away. Probably not, though.

Bill sat between them.

—That must be Martin's son there, said his father. — The tall lad fussing with the mass cards on the coffin.

—Martin wasn't a tall man.

—He was.

—Not that tall, said Bill's mother.

—No, said his father.—But that seems to be the way. They get taller and taller. Each generation. Look at Billy's gang. Great tall girls.

—Is that a daughter up there now?

—Or a wife.

—That hair's natural, I'd say. The colour.

—Natural or no, she's a good-looking lassie.

—Lovely, said his mother.—It's lovely to see.

The church was filling up.

—He got a good crowd, said Bill's father.

His mother sat forward. She was looking at the altar, the side opposite the coffin. A door had opened and people in front of him were beginning to stand. He saw an altar boy walk out before bodies got in the way and he stood up too. He heard his father groan as he stood. He watched his mother's hands grip the bench in front of her. He looked up, and saw the priest. He'd gone across the front of the altar and he was shaking hands with the people in the front row, the widow, the children, grandchildren. Bill looked quickly at his mother. She was fine – relaxed, curious.

The mass started and people sat. Bill tried to get rid of the terror, the fierce guilt that had a sore hold of his stomach. He glanced at his father. He looked fine, alert; he seemed to be enjoying himself. He looked at his mother. She was there again – his mother – leaning forward, watching, her lips moving very slightly. Bill sat between them, afraid to let his arms and shoulders touch either of them; the contact would push something, a button, a memory. The priest was young, in his thirties, but he went through the lines like an older man. He didn't even recite them. The voice was a drone; Bill only heard the words because he'd known them all his life. The tan was even stranger. It was dark in the church but the altar was well lit and your man, the priest, had definitely been under a lamp or had gone at himself with a can of false tan. The vestments were purple; the skin was orange. *Chasuble*. The word popped open. The name of the priest's purple cape. It had been there in Bill's head, waiting. Thirty years. Forty. *Alb. Stole*. He couldn't see the priest's shoes. He wondered were they proper black, hoped they weren't. He'd give the man a pair of Keds. *A priest wearing Keds. At a funeral*. He wasn't sure what Keds were. He'd heard the girls, his daughters, talking about them. Something about gay men wearing Keds. He liked the name. He'd put a pair on the priest. Orange ones, to go with the tan.

She was there again. The stranger. Her elbow went into Bill's ribs as she stood up, fell back, stood, gripped the bench, like she wanted to snap the wood, break through the back of the pew.

He was going to pull her back. He'd gently grab her, try to get her out.

Everyone else was standing now, obeying some command he'd missed.

She was growling. He could hear her, under the Apostles' Creed. *He suffered under Pontius Pilate, was crucified, died and was buried*. She growled – there were no words. There was no one looking at her yet. The bench, at her other side, was empty. There was no one right behind them. Bill was ready now to grab her arm. He looked at his father. He nudged him.

—What?

His father shouted. *He will come again to judge the living and the dead.*

—Ma isn't well, said Bill.

—Oh.

His father leaned out, looked at Bill's mother.

—Right.

He moved, along the pew, to the centre aisle. Bill thought his father would trip over – there was hardly any room for his feet. But he made it to the aisle. He started to genuflect. He was shaking slightly – Bill thought. But he was fine. He'd straightened up, steadied himself. He was turning away from the altar and the coffin.

Bill made himself do it: he put his hand on his mother's arm. He squeezed gently, pulled gently.

—What's wrong? she said.

She looked fine; she was his mother. He thought about calling his father back.

—Da's not feeling well, he said.

He moved, and she came with him. He let go of her sleeve.

—Excuse me, sorry – thanks.

His mother was beside him, in against him. He smiled at people he didn't know. He looked at the ground.

They were out.

His father was there.

—Alright, love?

He moved to meet Bill's mother as she came off the last step.

—I'm fine, she said.—Are *you* alright?

—I'm fine. We're both fine.

—I'll look after you.

—Good girl. I know you will.

They stood beside each other.

—They won't touch you.

—No, said Bill's father.—They won't. Not with you minding me.

The rain was starting, hard drops that blackened the ground around them.

—Will we get in the car? said Bill.

He wanted to get sick. He really did. Thinking – trying not to think – about what he'd just learnt, what he might have learnt. His father as a boy. Bill couldn't remember his grandmother's house, the house his father had grown up in. He couldn't really remember his grandmother either. A bottle of red lemonade and a Club Milk – they were all he could remember clearly, the only things he could see. Sitting at a table, the kitchen. His chin resting on the table; he was very small, very young. His granny was off to the right, on the other side of the table. She wasn't sitting; she was busy. She was talking to other people. Her back, and grey hair. That was all Bill had. His mother was sitting there too. His father was some- where else. Bill remembered where: he was down the street, visiting a cousin. But he couldn't remember his granny. He knew he'd liked her – he'd loved her. He knew he'd liked going there. He couldn't remember her funeral. He didn't know if he'd been at it.

—Alright, Billy-boy?

His father was looking at him.

—Yeah, said Bill. —Yeah. We'll get into the car.

—Good idea. Come on, love.

Bill went at their pace, across the car park. He clicked the doors open before they got to the car. He opened his father's door, his mother's.

—Good man.

His mother slid in. His father closed the front passenger door and bent down at his mother's door.

—Scoot in there, he told her.

He stood, so he could look at Bill over the car roof. Bill could see the pain in the eyes as his father straightened his back.

—I'll get in beside your mother, he said.—You'll be alright on your own.

—I'll be grand, said Bill.

He waited till his father was sitting inside – he didn't want to hear the groans – then he got in behind the wheel and wiped the rain from his face.

He looked in the rear-view mirror.

—What now? he said.

—What's that?

—Where to?

They both looked small and lost back there.

—Home, I think, said his father.—What d'you say, love?

She nodded.

—It's a bit wet for the graveyard, she said.

There were bubbles and cracks in her voice, as if some of the rain had got into it.

—Right, said Bill. —I'll get started, so we can have some heat.

—Good man.

Bill trusted his hands, his arms, his control of the wheel. The wipers cleared the rain off the windscreen. His stomach was grand; he felt safer in the car. The noise of the engine, the wipers and the heater filled the hole.

Wexford. He reminded himself – he had to; that was where they were. His mother had growled in the church. She'd told him his father had been abused by a priest – he thought she had.

He looked in the rear-view again.

—Do you have your belts on?

They were sitting apart now, a window each.

—I do.

—I forgot, hang on.

His father muttered.

—Bloody thing.

Then he looked at Bill's eyes in the mirror.

—All set here now.

—Fine, said Bill. —Here we go.

It was easy-going, good roads, the new motorway. The rain didn't matter. He turned down the heat. He said nothing for a while; they said nothing. He turned on the radio, changed his mind, turned it off. They didn't object. He looked in the mirror

—I'm sorry.

It was his mother. She'd seen his eyes.

—Why? said Bill – and his father.

—I spoilt your day.

—You didn't.

—Not at all.

—I think I probably did.

—No.

—It all came back, she said.

Bill watched his father nod – once, twice. His father's hand was there now, resting on his mother's shoulder.

—A terrible time, said his mother, to Bill; she was looking at the mirror. There was a truck far ahead, nothing else. Nothing behind him.

—It was, said his father.

—But I rescued you, she said.

—That's right.

—He was in the Artane Boys' Home, his mother told the mirror.

Something had happened. Suddenly – as fast as it took him to check that the road ahead was still clear – Bill knew he didn't have to believe this. He didn't have to change his past.

—We broke down the wall, she said. —We blew it up.

—That's right.

—They were making him play the tin whistle, she said.—For that band they had. The boys' band.

—It was torture, said his father.

Bill looked at the father. He was looking at Bill's mother.

—But we shot them all, she said.

—That's right.

—I shot most of them.

—I'll never forget it. The bullets were hopping.

Bill looked at her, at him. They were crying, both of them. Moved to tears by memories of things that could never have happened. *Jesus Christ*, he thought, *they've slipped into it together*.

—The way you burst in, said his father.—You should have seen her, Billy.

—They had big leather straps, she said.—The priests.

—They were Brothers, said his father.

—They were making you play the tin whistle.

—Absolute torture.

—It's a horrible instrument.

—Even in the right hands, said Bill's father.—But you came and saved me.

—Your poor lips were chapped.

The stories were going to get better. For a while. Bill watched his father wipe his eyes with a white handkerchief. Then, he supposed – Bill supposed – the funerals were going to stop. They wouldn't know who'd died. Or he'd be bringing them to the funerals of men and women who'd never existed. He hadn't noticed it starting. The decline, the slide. There must have been signs – things his mother had said, or his father. Bill had missed them, or ignored them.

It was quiet. He looked in the rear-view. They were both awake.

—Will I stop at the chipper? he asked.

—Oh, do, said his mother.

—That's where we went after your mother rescued me, said his father.—D'you remember that, love?

114

The roundabout was ahead. The end of the motorway, the beginning of Dublin.

—That's right, said his mother.—They watered the horses for us as well.

—I'd forgotten about that, said Bill's father.—You're right.

Bill looked in the rear-view. His father was staring back at Bill, waiting. He winked.

Blood

He grew up in Dracula's city. He'd walked past Bram Stoker's house every day on his way to school. But it had meant nothing to him. He'd never felt a thing, not the hand of a ghost or a shiver, not a lick on his neck, as he passed. In fact, he was nearly eighteen, in his last year at school, before he'd even noticed the plaque beside the door. He'd never read the book, and probably never would. He'd fallen asleep during Coppola's *Dracula*. One minute his wife was screaming, grabbing his knee; the next, she was grabbing the same knee, trying to wake him up. The cinema lights were on and she was furious.

—How can you do that?

—What?

—Sleep during a film like that.

—I always fall asleep when the film's shite.

—We're supposed to be out on a date.

—That's a different point, he said.—For that, I apologise. How did it end, anyway?

—Oh, fuck off, she said, affectionately – that was possible in Dublin.

So the whole thing, the whole Dracula business, meant absolutely nothing to him.

Nevertheless, he wanted to drink blood.

Badly.

The *badly* was recent, and dreadful. The itch, the urge, the leaking tongue – it was absolutely dreadful.

He wasn't sure when it had started. He was, though – he knew when he'd become aware.

—How d'you want your steak?

—Raw.

His wife had laughed. But he'd been telling her the truth. He wanted the slab of meat she was holding over the pan, raw and *now* – fuck the pan, it wasn't needed. He could feel muscles holding him back, and other muscles fighting for him – neck muscles, jaw muscles.

Then he woke.

But he was awake already, still standing in the kitchen, looking at the steak, and looking forward to it.

—Rare, so, he said.

She smiled at him.

—You're such a messer, she said.

He hid behind that, the fact that he acted the eejit, that it was *him*, as he bent down to the charred meat on the plate a few minutes later, and licked it. The kids copied him and they all ended up with brown gravy on their noses. He made himself forget about his aching jaws and the need to bite and growl. They all watched a DVD after dinner, and everything was grand.

And it was; it was fine. Life was normal. For a while. For quite a while. Weeks – he thought. He opened the fridge one day. There were two fillet steaks on a plate, waiting. It must have been weeks later because she – her name was Vera – she wouldn't have bought steak all that frequently. And it wasn't the case that Vera did all the shopping, or even most of it; she just went past the butcher's more often than he did. She bought the food; he bought the wine. She bought the soap and toilet paper – and he bought the wine. *You're such a messer.*

He grabbed one of the steaks and took it over to the sink. He looked behind him, to make sure he was alone, and then devoured it as he leaned over the sink. But he didn't *devour* it. He licked it first, like an ice pop; it was cold. He heard the drops of blood hit the aluminium beneath him, and he felt the blood running down his chin, as if it – the blood – was coming from him. And he started to suck it, quickly, to drink it. It should have been warm. He knew that, and it disgusted him, the fact that he was already planting his disappointment, setting himself up to do it again – *this* – feeding a need, an addiction he suddenly had and accepted. He growled – he fuckin' growled. He looked behind him – but he didn't care. *You're such a messer.* He chewed till it stopped being meat and spat the pulp into the bin. He rubbed his chin; he washed his hands. He looked at his shirt. It was clean. He ran the hot tap and watched the black drops turn red, pink, then nothing. He took the remaining fillet from the fridge and slid it off the plate, into the bin. He tied the plastic liner and brought it out to the wheelie bin.

—Where's the dinner? Vera wanted to know, later.

—What?

—I bought fillet steaks for us. There.

She stood in front of the fridge's open door.

—They were off, he said.

—They were not.

—They were, he said.—They were minging. I threw them out.

—They were perfect, she said.—Are they in here?

She was at the bin.

—The wheelie, he said.

He hadn't expected this; he hadn't thought ahead.

—I'm bringing them back, she said, as she moved to the back door.—The fucker.

She was talking about the butcher.

—Don't, he said.

He didn't stand up, he didn't charge to block her. He stayed sitting at the table. He could feel his heart – his own meat – hopping, thumping.

—He's always been grand, he said.—If we complain, it'll – I don't know – change the relationship. The customer–client thing.

He enjoyed listening to himself. He was winning.

—We can have the mince, he said.

—It was for the kids, she said.—Burgers.

—I like burgers, he said.—You like burgers.

119

The back door was open. It was a hot day, after a week of hot days. He knew: she didn't want to open the wheelie and shove her face into a gang of flies.

They had small burgers. The kids didn't complain.

That was that.

Out of his system. He remembered – he saw himself – attacking the meat, hanging over the sink. He closed his eyes, snapped them shut – the idea, the thought, of being caught like that. By a child, by his wife. The end of his life.

He'd killed it – the urge. But it came back, days later. And he killed it again. The fridge again – lamb chops this time. He sent his hand in over the chops, and grabbed a packet of chicken breasts, one of those polystyrene trays, wrapped in cling-film. He put a finger through the film, pulled it away. He slid the breasts onto a plate – and drank the pink, the near-white blood. He downed it, off the tray. And vomited.

Cured. Sickened – revolted. Never again. He stayed home from work the next day. Vera felt his forehead.

—Maybe it's the swine flu.

—Chickenpox, he said. *You're such a messer.*

—You must have had the chickenpox when you were a boy, she said.—Did you?

—I think so, he said.

She looked worried.

—It can make adult males sterile, she said.

—I had a vasectomy, he told her. —Three years ago.

—I forgot, she said.

—I didn't.

120

But he was cured; he'd sorted himself out. The thought, the memory – the taste of the chicken blood, the polystyrene tray – it had him retching all day. He wouldn't let it go. He tortured himself until he knew he was fixed.

It was iron he was after. He decided that after he'd done a bit of googling when he went back to work. It made sense; it was fresh air across his face. Something about the taste, even the look, of the cow's deep red blood – it was metal, rusty. That was what he'd craved, the iron, the metal. He'd been looking pale; he'd been falling asleep in front of the telly, like an old man. Anaemia. Iron was all he needed. So he bought himself a carton of grapefruit juice – he knew the kids would never touch it – and he went into a chemist's on his way home from work, for iron tablets. He regretted it when the woman behind the counter looked at him over her specs and asked him if they were for his wife.

—We share them, he said.

She wasn't moving.

—I'd need to see a letter from your GP, she said.

—For iron?

—Yes.

He bought condoms and throat lozenges, and left. By the time he got home he knew his iron theory was shite and he'd pushed the grapefruit juice into a hedge, with the condoms. The kids were right: grapefruit juice was disgusting. There was nothing wrong with him, except he wanted to drink blood.

He had kids. That was the point. A boy and a girl.

He had a family, a wife he loved, a job he tolerated. He worked in one of the banks, not high enough up to qualify for one of the mad bonuses they'd been handing out in the boom days, but high enough to have his family held hostage while he went to the bank with one of the bad guys and opened the safe – although that event had never occurred. The point was, he was normal. He was a forty-one-year-old heterosexual man who lived in Dublin and enjoyed the occasional pint with his friends – Guinness; loads of iron – played a game of indoor football once a week in a leaking school hall, had sex with his wife often enough to qualify as regularly, just about, and would like to have had sex with other women, many other women, but it was just a thought, never a real ambition or anything urgent or mad. He was normal.

He took a fillet steak into the gents' toilet at work, demolished it, and tried to flush the plastic bag down the toilet. But it stayed there like a parachute on top of the water. He fished it out and put it in his pocket. He checked his shirt and tie in the mirror, even though he'd been careful not to let himself get carried away as he went at the meat in the cubicle. He was clean, spotless, his normal self. He checked his teeth for strings of flesh, put his face right up to the mirror. He was grand. He went back to his desk and ate his lunch with his colleagues, a sandwich he'd made himself that morning, avocado and tomato – no recession in his fridge. He felt good, he felt great.

He was controlling it, feeding it. He was his own

doctor, in very good hands. He'd soon be ironed up and back to his even more normal self.

So he was quite surprised when he went over the wall, even as he went over. *What the fuck am I doing?* He knew exactly what he was doing. He was going after the next-door neighbours' recession hens. At three in the morning. He was going to bite the head off one of them. He'd seen the hens – he wasn't sure if you called them hens or chickens – from one of the upstairs windows. He saw them every night when he was closing his daughter's curtains, after he'd read to her. (See? He's normal.) There were three of them, scrabbling around in the garden. He hated them, the whole idea of them. The world economy wobbled and the middle classes immediately started growing their own spuds and carrots, buying their own chickens, and denying they had property portfolios in Eastern Europe. And they stopped talking to him because he'd become the enemy, and evil, because he worked in a bank. The shiftless bitch next door could pretend she was busy all day looking after the hens. Well, she'd have one less to look after because he was over the wall. He'd landed neatly and quietly – he was fit; he played football – and he was homing in on the hens.

He knew what he was up to. He was hoping a light would go on, upstairs – or better, downstairs – or next door, in his own house. Frighten the shite out of him, send him scrambling back over the wall. *I was just looking to see if I could see the Space Shuttle. It's supposed to be coming over Ireland tonight.* He'd bluff his way out of it – *Although it won't be stopping* – while his heart thumped away at his ribs. It would sort him out for another few days, a week; it would get him over the weekend.

But no light went on.

And the chickens cluck-clucked. *We're over here*.

He grabbed one. It was easy, too easy. It was a lovely night; they were as clear there as they could have been, standing in a row, like a girl band, the Supremes. Shouldn't they have been cooped up – was that the phrase? – and let out again in the morning? The city's foxes were famous; everyone had seen one. He'd seen one himself, strolling down the street when he was walking home from the station a few months before.

He grabbed his hen, expected the protest, the pecks. But no, the hen settled into his arms like a fuckin' kitten. The little head in one hand, the hard, scrawny legs in the other, he stretched it out like a rubber band and brought it up to his mouth. And he bit – kind of. There was no burst of blood or even a clean snap. The neck was still in his mouth. He could feel a pulse on his tongue. The hen was terrified; he could feel that in the legs. But he didn't want to terrify the bird – he wasn't a cruel man. He just wanted to bite its head off and hold his mouth under its headless neck. But he knew: he didn't have it in him. He wasn't a vampire or a were-wolf. And he needed a filling – he could feel that. *I was biting the head off a chicken, doctor*. He'd put the hen down now and get back over the wall.

But a light went on – and he bit. Downstairs, right

in front of him – and the head came clean off. There was no blood, not really, just – well – bone, gristle, something wet. He wouldn't vomit. They'd be staring out at him, the neighbours, him or her or him *and* her – Jim and Barbara. But he was quick, he was calm. He knew they couldn't see him because the light was on in the kitchen and it was dark out here. Although, now that he thought of it – and he *was* thinking – they might have seen him before they turned on the light.

And now the chicken, the headless, dead chicken, decided to protest. A squawk came out of something that couldn't have been its beak, because the head, detached or at least semi-detached, was in one of his hands. He was holding the body by the neck and it was wriggling. *Let me down, let me down.*

He dropped the hen, heard it running away, and he charged. He ran at the wall. Not his own wall – he was *thinking*. The wall on the other side, two houses down from his own. He was up, no sweat, and he was over. He sat down for a while, to get his breath back, to work out his route home. He listened. He hadn't heard the kitchen door being opened and the hen seemed to have accepted that it was dead. The other two hadn't noticed, or they were in mourning. It was very quiet.

He was safe – he thought he was safe. He was stupid, exhilarated, appalled, ashamed, fuckin' delighted, and safe. He looked up at the sky. And he saw it, the Shuttle. The brightest star, moving steadily across the night. The *Endeavour* – he remembered the name.

He was back in the bed.

She woke – half woke. His cold feet, his weight on the mattress.

—What's wrong?

—Nothing, he said.—I got up to see the Shuttle.

—Great.

She was asleep already.

—It was amazing, he said, addressing her back.— Amazing.

He kissed her neck.

He actually slept. It was Friday night, Saturday morning. The bed was empty when he woke. It was a long time since that had happened, since she'd been awake before him. He felt good – he felt great. He'd flossed and brushed before he'd got back into bed, no trace of the hen between his teeth. He'd gargled quietly till his eyes watered. No bad taste, and no guilt. He shouldn't have done what he'd done, but a more important consideration quickly smothered any guilt. It was the thought he'd fallen asleep with, clutching it like a teddy bear, just after he'd kissed his wife's neck.

Necks.

It was as simple as that.

The blood was a red herring, so to speak, sent to distract him – by his psyche or whatever, his conscience – to stop him from seeing the much healthier obvious. It was necks he'd been craving, not blood. He didn't want to drink blood and he was no more anaemic than a cow's leg. The simple, dirty truth was he wanted to bite necks. It was one of those midlife things. And that was grand, it was fine, because he was in the middle of his life, give or take a few years.

Sex.

Simple.

He wanted to have sex with everything living. Not literally. He wanted to have sex with most things. Some things – most women. He was a normal man, slipping into middle age. His days were numbered. He knew this, but he didn't *think* it. A year was 365 days. Ten years was 3,650. Thirty years gave him 10,950. *You have 10,950 days to live. That's fine, thanks.* As he lay on the bed, he felt happy. The urge was gone, because he understood. His mind was fine, but something in him had been running amok. His biology, or something like that. Not long ago, only a few generations back, he'd have been dead already or at least drooling and toothless. Middle age and the autumn years were modern concepts. His brain understood them, but his biology – his manhood – didn't. He only had a few years of riding left: that was what biology thought. More to the point, a few years of reproducing. And maybe the vasectomy had made things worse, or more drastic, sent messages haywire – he didn't know.

The human mind was a funny thing. He'd been dying for a ride, so he bit the head off a neighbour's chicken.

He went downstairs.

—A fox got one of Barbara's hens last night, said Vera.

—Well, that was kind of inevitable, wasn't it?

—That's a bit heartless.

—It's what foxes do, he said.—When?

—What?

—When did the fox strike?

—Last night, she said.—Did you hear anything when you were looking at the Shuttle?

—Not a thing, he said.—Just the astronauts chatting. She smiled. *You're such a messer.*

—About what?

—Oh, just about how much they love Ireland. How's Barbara?

—In bits.

—Did she say she felt violated?

—She did, actually, but you're such a cynical bastard.

She was laughing. And he knew: he was home and dry.

It was later now, night again, and he kissed her neck. He bit her neck. They were a pair of kids for half an hour, and still giddy half an hour after that.

—Well, she said.—I'm ready for afters.

Her hand went exploring.

—Back in a minute, he said.

He went downstairs, went to the fridge – two mackerel on a plate. He looked in the freezer, pulled out a likely bag. A couple of pork chops. He put the bag under the hot tap, till the plastic loosened. Then he tore away the plastic and went at one of the chops. But it was too hard, too cold. He gave it thirty seconds in the microwave and hoped – and dreaded – that the ding would bring her downstairs. He stood at the kitchen window and nibbled at the edges of the chop and hoped – and dreaded

– that she'd come in and see his reflection – the blind was up – before she saw him, that he'd turn and reveal himself, some kind of vampire having a snack, and she'd somehow find it sexy or at least reasonable, and forgive him, and put her hands through his hair, like she did, and maybe even join him in the chop, and he'd bring her over the wall so they could get Barbara's last two hens, one each.

He binned the rest of the chop, shook the bin so it would disappear under the other rubbish.

He'd wait for the right moment. The visuals were important; there was a huge difference between being caught devouring raw steak and licking a frozen pork chop, or inviting your life partner to do the same. There was no hurry, no mad rush. No madness at all; he was normal.

He went back upstairs.

She was waiting for him. But not in the bed, or *on* the bed. She was standing far away from the bed.

—What's this? she asked.

She turned on the light.

She was holding a head on the palm of her open hand. A small head.

—A chicken's head, he said.

—Where did you get it?

—I found it.

He was a clown, an eejit; he'd hidden it under his socks.

—It's Barbara's, she said. —Isn't it?

—Barbara's head would be a bit bigger, he said.

It didn't work; she didn't smile.

—Did the fox drop it in the garden? she asked.

She was giving him an escape route, offering him a reasonable story. But it was the wrong one. He'd found a chicken's head and hidden it? He wasn't going to admit to the lie. It was sad, perverse.

—No, he said.

—Well, she said, and looked away.—What happened?

—I bit it off, he said.

She looked at him again. For quite a while.

—What was that like?

—Great, he said. —Great.

The Plate

—I love you but I think I'm dying.

This was what he said as he came in the back door. Then he turned around and walked back out. Maeve thought he was leaving her. He'd said he was the night before. Until she saw the way he was walking. And she knew it: he *was* dying. He walked like he'd been stabbed, away from the door, out into the garden. It was after nine but still bright enough, early September. His back to her, crouched, he moved quickly, sideways, clutching something – his stomach. The back door was a slider, all glass. She watched him move down the garden. She waited for him to fall. She waited for the blood.

But he didn't fall.

—Are you alright?

She stayed at the door.

—Jim?

He'd gone to the end of the garden. The sun was down, behind the high back wall. He was dark, crouched, still moving. She saw now; he was coming back.

131

—Are you okay?

She moved towards him.

—No, he said.

—Who stabbed you?

—What?

He looked down at his hands, at the way he was holding himself.

There was no blood. She could see that. And that made it worse, more serious – internal.

—I wasn't stabbed, he said.

—What's wrong?

—I'm dying, he said.—I don't know.

He couldn't stand straight; he didn't try. The pain was unbelievable. Literally that – unbelievable. He had to move, keep moving; that was all he knew.

—Will I phone for a doctor?

She heard herself and knew how stupid it sounded.

—Or an ambulance? Jim?

He was walking away again, back down the garden. Crouching. He didn't answer.

He hadn't felt good all day. But that was all. There'd been the hangover but that was gone by late morning, before twelve. Then he'd realised there was something more, something wrong, nudging at him, in his groin. He wasn't sure exactly what the *groin* was, where it started and ended. Somewhere in below his stomach, there was something poking at him, or stuck. Nothing too bad, nothing to make him think that he wasn't well or that he'd soon be dead.

Maeve didn't bother with the phone. She could hear

herself trying to explain it to their GP, a waste of time. She grabbed the car keys and went back out to Jim. She locked the back door.

—Jim.

It was darker now. She couldn't see if he'd heard her.

—Jim.

—What?

It didn't sound like him.

—Come on, she said.

—What?

—We'll go to the hospital.

—Which one?

—You're dying, for God's sake. Does it matter?

—Yes, it does, he said.

He knew, as he spoke. He probably wasn't dying. He felt robbed.

The nurse took a look at him, bent over, holding onto the side of the trolley, and she told him.

—That's a kidney stone.

—Is it serious?

—You'll be grand.

He knew what it was now, and the pain stayed bad but bearable.

—There'll be a doctor around in a minute, she said.

He got up on the trolley and tried to lie back. He held onto the bars and thought his heat would melt them. The place was packed and dreadful but the nurse came back with a doctor who, without the white lab coat, would have looked like a kid who filled bags in a

133

supermarket. He pressed Jim's stomach and told him nothing, but gave him a jab, some sort of painkiller.

Ten minutes later, the pain was there but lurking behind a soft wall. Jim could breathe and try to get comfortable. But he was in hell and he'd never recover. The nurse or the doctor, probably the doctor, had left the curtain open. Jim watched a junkie die. A girl, on a trolley. Her pals, two skinny girls in tracksuits, screamed and forgot about her, and screamed again.

—Tracey!

A security guard pushed them out. He seemed to know them. They came back in, up the wheelchair ramp, and screamed again and lit their smokes and got thrown out. Jim watched the ambulance men give up, and put the blanket over the dead girl's face, and they wheeled her away somewhere. Her friends came in, sat in two orange bucket seats and fell asleep. While the girl died and disappeared, a woman near him moaned, men puked, a guy who seemed to have lost a hand, or at least the fingers – the bandage was huge and blood-soaked – tried to eat a bag of crisps. Jim closed his eyes but it didn't work. The noise alone was worse; he had to watch. He'd never sleep. He wanted to be rescued.

The night before, the Thursday, they'd had a fight. Another one. A fight they drank into. It was fuelled by the red wine they knocked back before they ate and as they ate. The third glass brought Jim up to date; he caught up with the state he'd been in the night before. The edges he'd carried all day were gone and he was back where he'd left off, where he'd lost interest or consciousness – he couldn't remember. One minute they were chatting away carefully – his day, her day – and then, like that, he knew it was all shite. They sat with the plates on their laps – they didn't have a table. He listened to something about her mother's aunt, a fall in the shower; some old woman he'd met once, two years before at the wedding. He listened for a while – because that was what he did, that was what *you* did. The aunt's broken leg equalled two of his funny incidents at work.

—You're not listening.

—I am.

—You're not.

—I am. Your auntie broke her leg. Go on.

—No.

—Go on. She slid on the soap.

—You're a callous bastard.

—I didn't put the soap there.

—Everything's a laugh, she said.

She put her plate on the floor so she could get to her glass.

He said nothing.

—Everything has to be a laugh.

—She slid on the soap, he said. —Go on. I'm all ears. Was it Palmolive or Lifebuoy?

She stared at him.

—You're such a prick, she said.

—Will she be okay? he asked.

The question surprised her – he could tell. She bent down for her plate. He was winning.

—You don't care, she said.

—I do.

—You don't.

—I can't fuckin' win, can I?

She sighed. She put a fork-load into her mouth. He watched her eating. Chicken curry.

She sighed again.

—Okay, she said.—You win.

—Win what?

—Whatever you want.

—This is ridiculous.

—Everything's ridiculous, she said.

—You said it.

—Yeah.

It was the same row, and the same conclusion. He cornered her. She cried; sometimes he cried. He believed everything he said, although he'd no idea now what they'd been arguing about, or if it had been a proper argument; it was gone. But this was it, every night – most nights.

But the plate was new. It landed at his feet, and then he saw her throw it, after it hit the floor – her movement made sense, and her face. She held the plate like a Frisbee, then sent it his way and regretted it. Her other hand tried to catch it. It landed flat and it didn't break.

He leaned out of his chair and banged his heel down on it.

—There, he said.—That's how you break a plate.

But it wasn't broken. And he didn't try again. The

back of his shoe and his trouser cuff were covered in the curry.

She laughed.

Friday night, in the back garden, he was walking again. He had to keep moving, outrun the pain.

—It depends which of the hospitals is on call, he said, as he went back down the garden.—If it's Beaumont, okay. But Blanchardstown. Too far. I'll never make it.

This was in 1990, at the tail end of the last recession. There wasn't enough money to keep all the hospitals open.

—I'll check, she said.

She went back in and got the phone book out from under all the other crap. She found the number for Beaumont, the nearest hospital to them. She could even hear a siren outside as she dialled, an ambulance on its way there, or coming from there. Someone else dying.

He heard it too. Was it coming for him?

He could think. He wasn't dying. There was something seriously wrong but it wasn't getting worse. As long as he kept moving.

She was back out. He watched her lock the back door.

—The Mater, she said.

—On call?

—Yeah.

—Where's the ambulance gone?

—What ambulance?

—I heard one.

She was holding his arm, moving him off the grass.

—That was for someone else, she said.—I'm driving you in. It'll be quicker.

She'd had nothing to drink. Nothing all day.

—I don't know, he said.

They were off the grass, at the side of the house. Behind the car.

—What?

—If I can sit in the car, he said.

—We have to get you there, she said.

She'd unlocked the passenger door, still holding his arm.

She helped him in; he felt her fingers on his neck.

—Thanks.

—It's okay, you're fine.

He couldn't sit properly. He couldn't sit back, or put on his belt. She got the car started, reversed slowly out, then straightened the car and headed for the main road.

—How's it going?

—Okay.

—Won't be long.

There was no traffic; they met nothing on the roundabout.

—I don't know if I can do this, he said.—Sorry.

His hand was on the handle of the door.

—Don't!

—What?

—Open the door!

—I wasn't going to.

She drove off the roundabout and looked in the rear-view mirror.

—Oh Christ!

—What?

—The baby!

—Oh Jesus, oh sweet Jesus.

—The baby.

—It'll be grand. Turn back.

He couldn't believe it. They'd forgotten the baby. It was horrible. But the shock wasn't that they'd forgotten. The real shock was that they'd never thought.

The baby. It – *she* didn't even have a name. That wasn't true, of course. The baby did have a name. Holly was the baby's name and pretending she didn't have a name was just some sort of weird sentimentality. As the car went over a pothole and the jolt shifted whatever was inside killing him – the blade out and straight back in – he knew it was just self-pity. He loved the baby. *They* loved the baby. He was dying, and they'd forgotten to bring her with them. That was all.

—She'll be grand, he said. —We only left her a few minutes.

—Yeah, she said.

They were back on the roundabout, and off the round-about, a minute from home; the road was clear. And he knew something, in the minute it took to get to the house: they were happy.

The Dog

She'd been gone for a couple of hours, most of the afternoon – he wasn't sure – but she looked like she'd been in Spain. Or the Sahara. She'd been tied down and tortured, under a big round sun. She was suddenly tanned.

He watched her taking off her coat. He didn't know what colour her hair was, the name for it. He sat still and said nothing.

It went back.

They hadn't coped well. He knew that.

His ear had been the start of it. Or a start. Years ago now. Mary had been kissing him. But she'd stopped and he'd heard something, trapped in her throat.

—What's wrong? he'd said.

—Nothing, she'd said.—Your ear.

She'd stiffened beside him, but then he felt her kind of unfold, relax again.

—My ear?

—There's a hair on it.

—Hair? he said.—There's hair in everyone's ear.

—On, she said.

—What?

—It's *on* your ear.

—On?

He saw her nod.

—I'll have to see this, he said, and got up.

But he couldn't see it. He put his face right up to the bathroom mirror. He turned his head, so his ear was nearly the only thing he could see. But he couldn't see a hair. He took off his glasses. And he saw it. All on its own. At the bottom, the lobe. Like a moustache hair. He put the glasses back on. The hair was gone. He took them off. And there it was.

He went back to the bedroom. He got into the bed. She was pretending to be asleep, breathing like a baby in an ad.

He dated it back to then. Five years, four years – he wasn't sure. When they stopped growing old together.

He'd shaved it off. He'd never had a moustache and he didn't want one now, growing on his ear. He'd taken his glasses off to do it – he'd had to. He needed the glasses but sometimes he could see better without them. He took them off to read the paper. He had to put them on to find the fuckin' paper.

She was still taking her coat off. It looked new. He didn't think he'd seen it on her before. It was nice, soft-looking. He didn't know what to call the colour of that, either. She was being careful. It must have been new. He said nothing.

Her knickers came after his ear. His revenge, he supposed, but he hadn't meant it that way. It had just happened. He'd been sitting up in the bed, reading. *Berlin: The Downfall 1945*, or *Stalingrad* – one of those big books he always liked, about a city getting hammered in the Second World War. He loved history. He could hear her locking the doors downstairs, and coming up the stairs, shoving the bedroom door open, coming in. It must have been the Stalingrad book, because he'd got to the bit about people eating the rats, and he'd looked away from the page. She was taking her jeans off, her back to him. She was kind of vague there, so he put his glasses back on, and saw them. Her knickers – her thong. New, and black. She was bending, to get her feet out of the jeans. Four decades of arse parked inside a piece of string.

He pretended he was going to vomit. He still regretted it. He made the gagging sound, and leaned over the side of the bed and let on he was emptying himself. He'd done it before, and she'd always laughed. Not this time.

He hadn't meant to hurt her. He'd thought he was just being funny. She'd said nothing about it.

He googled *menopause*, but he soon gave up. *Age of onset, cessation of menses*; it was boring. *Hot flushes* – he had one of them every time he went up the stairs. But he kept an eye on her. He clucked sympathetically when he saw her sweating. He brought her a glass of water and put it beside the bed. She stared at him before she thanked him.

*   *   *

The chest hair was next. His. He woke up sweating one morning. The room was bright. The sun was already pushing through the curtains. She was leaning right over him, looking straight down at his chest.

—Grey, she said.

—What?

There was something there, a pain – the memory. She'd done something to him while he was asleep.

—There's grey in your hair.

He was sure of it. She'd pulled the hair on his chest. She looked now like she was going to peck him, the way she was hanging there. It felt like she already had.

—Did you pull my hair? he said.

He could hear himself ask the question, almost like he wasn't the one talking. He wasn't sure he was awake.

She didn't answer.

—And white, she said.

—Did you?

—What?

—Pull my hair.

—What? Why would I do that?

She said it like she was miles away, or on the phone to someone else. Someone she didn't think much of.

He got up on one of his elbows. He looked down at his chest; he tried to see it properly. His eyes swam a bit. Her back was to him; she was getting up. She held her nightdress down as she stood out of the bed.

—It's not really something you think about, is it? she said. —What happens you when you get older.

She was standing now, looking behind the curtain, out the window.

—It's a bit horrible, she said.

—It's only hair.

He'd had grey hair for a good while. It had started in his early thirties, on his head. A few at the side, just above his ears. She'd liked it; so she'd said. She'd said it made him look distinguished. A bit like Bill Clinton. You expected the hair on your head to change; you knew it was coming. But not the chest hair, or the pubic stuff. So she was right; it was a bit horrible.

He'd examined himself that morning. He'd looked no different. He took his glasses off so he could look at his face properly. He was still there, the same man. It was frightening, though, how little time you got. You only became yourself when you were twenty-three or twenty-four. A few years later, you had an old man's chest hair. It wasn't worth it. He put his glasses back on.

He didn't decide to throw out the statue. One of the saints – he couldn't remember which one, a woman. A present from one of her aunts. He'd just picked it up, walking past it in the hall. Kept walking, into the kitchen, threw it in the bin. Tied the bag, brought it out to the wheelie, dropped it in. Went back to the kitchen and put a new biodegradable bag into the bin. The mark was there on the table, where the statue had been; the varnish was much darker, like a badge – 'Something Used To Be Here'. She'd never asked about it; she'd never said anything. He'd never felt guilty. She'd never tried to cover the mark; she'd never rearranged the crap on the table, and neither had he.

But she'd thrown out his medal. Not that he gave a fuck. But she had.

The statue first. They'd both laughed at it, when the aunt was in the taxi, going home, the night she'd given it to them. The saint's big blue eyes, the snakes at her plaster feet. He'd put it on the table in the hall; he'd made room for it. It was him who'd done it. He'd made a ceremony of it. This was the first Christmas they'd been in the house, two years after the wedding. They'd laughed, and she'd kissed him.

He just picked it up and threw it in the bin. He didn't know he was going to do it. He just did. He'd often hoped she'd ask him about it, because he could have told her. It could have been the beginning of something; they'd have talked. But she didn't, and he didn't.

The medal. It was the only one he'd ever won. The Community Games, football. Under-10s. North Dublin. Runners-up. He remembered the final, losing three–nil, and not caring once he had the medal. And not caring much about the medal either. His mother had put it away, in the glass cabinet in the front room. She'd given it to him when he'd moved into his own house, along with all his old school reports and his Inter and Leaving Certs, and a few photographs: the team in their stripy jerseys, him at the front, smiling and freezing; him and his big sister on the back of a donkey-and-cart, both of them squinting; him in his first suit, the flared trousers, grinning and squinting, the day before his first real job. He could remember his father with the camera. 'Smile, smile. Stop bloody squinting.' He'd told his father to fuck off and walked straight out to the street. He could remember the noise of the trouser legs rubbing against each other.

She hadn't taken anything else. Just the medal. He hadn't been looking for it. He'd just noticed it, gone. He'd kept the stuff his mother gave him in the big envelope she'd put it into, with 'Joe' in her shaky writing on it. He'd kept it in a drawer in the bedroom, under socks and T-shirts. Over the years, the shape of the medal had been pressed into the paper of the envelope. Not the little footballer, or the '1969', or any of the other details. Just the circular shape. He'd been looking for a sock to match another one, and – he didn't know why – he'd put his finger on the circle and realised there was nothing under it. He took out the envelope and opened it. The medal was gone.

He searched the drawer. More than once. He took everything out. He shook all the socks. He slid the whole lot out of the envelope, and put it all back, one thing at a time. He tried the other drawers. He pulled the chest of drawers away from the wall and looked behind it. He took all the drawers out to see if the medal had slipped to the side, if it was standing on its edge on one of the plywood slats that held the drawers in place.

He put everything back.

He had no doubt at all: she'd done it.

But then the dog came into the house. They got a dog. She got the dog. A Jack Russell, a thoroughbred, papers and all. A mad little thing. It was there yapping at his heels when he got home from work.

—What's this? he said.

—What's it look like?

—A dog.

—There you go.

—Whose is it?

—Ours, she said.—Mine.

—Serious?

—Yeah.

He looked down at it.

—Let go of me fuckin' trousers, he said.

But he'd liked it, immediately. He'd had dogs when he was a kid. There'd always been a dog. Dogs were alright.

She gave it the name. Emma. From a book she liked, and the film, by Jane Austen. But it still ran around the kitchen in circles and knocked its head against the rungs beneath the chairs. It never stopped. It was always charging around the gaff, or asleep, beside its mat at the back door. Never on the mat, always right beside it. It was a great dog. Didn't shed too much hair, was too small to jump onto the good furniture, learnt to scratch at the door and yap when it wanted to get outside. Only shat in the kitchen now and again, and always looked apologetic. So, it was grand. But he soon began to realise that they weren't living with the same animal. She talked to it; she had a special voice she used. She'd buy a bag of jelly babies and share them, one for her, one for the dog. There was a child in the house, before he really understood.

He got up one morning and she was down there before him, filling the kettle. The dog had taken a dump beside the mat.

—Emma had an accident, she said.

—As long as it wasn't you, he said.

She laughed and he bent down, got the dog by the scruff, and pushed its snout into the shite. He unlocked the back door with his free hand and threw the dog outside, lobbed it gently, so it would land on its feet.

And she exploded. She actually hit him. She smacked him on the back, a loud whack that didn't hurt but shocked him. She hit him again. More of a thump this time – his shoulder.

—What was that for?

—What d'you think you're doing?

The two of them breathing hard.

He didn't hit her back. He didn't even think about it, or lift his hand or anything.

He knew immediately what she meant, and why she was furious. Now that she was. He could see.

—That's how you train them, he said.

—No, it isn't.

—It is.

It was how they'd trained their dogs at home, when he was a kid. Nose in the dirt, out the door. It had always worked.

—What other way is there?

He never mentioned the fact that she'd hit him. He never brought it up again, that the only one who'd ever been violent was her.

She signed them up for training classes. One evening a week, for eight weeks. They brought the dog to a big barn of a place, an actual barn beside an abandoned farmhouse, at the back of the airport. It was a strange, flat landscape. There was the ruin of a castle on one side of the road and the airport runway on the other, just a couple of fields away. He could look straight up at the bellies of the planes. The dog trainers were lovely, three soft-spoken girls who loved the dogs and the racket and the smell. He enjoyed it. They both did. The dog was quick on the uptake, all the sits and the stays, and she was fine with the other dogs. He enjoyed getting there, and coming home. They had to drive through Ballymun and over the M50 motorway. They'd comment on the changes, all the old tower blocks knocked down, the new buildings going up. There was once, on the road that ran right beside the runway, they saw something ahead – two things – getting clearer and sharper. It was two horses, pulling buggies, racing, on both sides of the road. He drove onto the hard shoulder, and they watched the horses trot past, and two Traveller kids in the buggies – they didn't even look at the car as they flew by.

—Jesus.
—That's disgraceful.
—Is it?
—It's dangerous.
—That's for sure.

He got out of the car – she did too – and they watched the buggies till they were too far away, waiting to see if any other cars or trucks came at them. But the road was empty.

—I wonder who won, she said.

—Don't know, he said.—A draw. I'd love to do it myself.

—Yeah, she said.—Not here, though.

—No.

They got back in and went on to the training centre.

Another time, they drove past a family of Romanians, gypsies, about seven of them, walking along the same road, beside the runway. It was like they'd just climbed over the perimeter fence and they were making a break for the city. But, really, they were strolling along and he'd no idea where to. He couldn't even imagine. There wasn't a shop or a house.

—Why would they want to be out here? she asked.

—Reminds them of home.

—Stop that.

—They're left alone out here, he said.—That's my guess.

—You're probably right, she said.—It's like a no-man's-land, isn't it?

—Yeah, he said.—It's nowhere.

—It's sad, though. Isn't it?

—I suppose it is.

Driving back home, after the training, they saw the Romanians again, off the road this time, on the island in the centre of the M50 roundabout; there were kids going into the bushes. He realised it slowly, and so did she. The car was off the roundabout and going through Ballymun before she spoke.

—They live in there, she said.

—What?

—The Romanians, she said.—They're living on the roundabout.

—It looked like it, alright.

—In the bushes.

—Yeah.

—Jesus.

—Yeah.

They brought the dog to the barn every Wednesday night, for the eight weeks. The dog could walk, stop, sit, stay and shit and there were no more rows or misunderstandings. She fed the dog. He picked the shit up off the grass in the back garden. And he brought the dog down to Dollymount strand for a run, on the mornings when he didn't have an early start. And those mornings were the best thing about having the dog. He'd park the car and walk towards the wooden bridge and the docks and the city behind it, and Dun Laoghaire to the left, across the bay, and the mountains. He saw herons one morning, two of them, standing still in the water. He'd never seen herons before; he hadn't even known that there were herons in Ireland. They didn't budge when the dog ran at them, until the last second. Then they were up together, and they flew off slowly, dragging their legs behind them, and they settled again, in the shallow water further down the beach. It thrilled him to see that. He loved the whole thing. Even when it rained – when the rain came at him sideways, straight off the sea, and he was soaking before he'd really started – he loved it. But he'd never have done it on his own. He'd never have been comfortable by himself, walking along the empty beach in the morning. He'd have felt strange. What was he doing there, all by himself? But with the dog it was fine. He didn't have to explain anything, to himself or to anyone else. He was walking the dog. Throwing a ball. Both of them getting their exercise.

Then the dog went missing.

He came home, and Mary was already there. Her eyes were huge and angry and terrified.

—You left the gate open.

—I didn't, he said.—What gate?

—The side gate.

—I didn't.

—It was open.

—I didn't touch it, he said.—Oh fuck, the dog.

He'd forgotten about the dog.

—I went out, she said.—I couldn't find her.

—She'll be grand, he said.—Hang on.

He went out to his car and came back with the street atlas. He divided the neighbourhood; he stayed calm. They'd get into their cars. She'd go right; he'd go left.

—She can't be gone too far.

He didn't believe that. He was already thinking about the next dog.

—D'you want a cup of tea before we go? he asked her.

He thought he was handling it well. She was crying. He wanted to hug her, but it was a long time since they'd done that. He knew she was angry. He'd look – he'd genuinely look for the dog. He'd stay out all night. He'd search everywhere. And he'd be delighted if he found it – he could feel it in his chest. But they'd been away all day. Nine hours. He'd left first – he remembered shouting 'Seeyeh' up the stairs, just before he'd closed the front door. But he hadn't been outside, in the back garden. He'd let the dog out – he remembered that. He'd been first down to the kitchen. The dog had stood up and stretched. He'd gone straight over to the door, to let her out. He'd had his coffee and his banana, and he'd gone. But the gate. He hadn't opened it. The night before? No. He couldn't remember touching the gate. It hadn't happened.

They went out to the cars together.

—What if she comes back when we're gone?

—It's not likely, is it?

—I just thought—

—I know, but she's never been out on her own before.

—I know.

—Let's stick to Plan A, he said.—What d'you think?

—Okay, she said.

He was looking at the side gate now, open.

—Would you prefer to stay here? he said.—In case.

—No, she said.—It's better if we both do it.

—Grand.

They didn't find the dog. He stayed out till after midnight. He drove past the house, twice, until he saw her car parked outside. Then he parked his own and went in.

—No luck?

—No, she said.

She didn't look at him. She was sitting at the kitchen table. Then she looked, and stopped.

—The bloody gate, she said.

—It wasn't me, he said.—I don't think it was. It isn't bin day.

—Bin day?

—Yeah. Bin day. The day in the week when I put out the bin. When I open the side gate. Every fuckin' week for the last twenty fuckin' years. Sorry.

He sat. He stood up. She looked at him.

—I'm sorry too, she said.

He sat.

—What'll we do?

—I don't know.

They went up to bed together and fell asleep, more or less, together. He was first out again in the morning. He didn't shout 'Seeyeh' up the stairs. He couldn't.

He hadn't opened the gate.

He looked at it before he started the car. It was still open. He got out of the car and shut it.

It was open again when he got home.

—In case Emma comes back, she told him.

—Oh, he said. —Fair enough.

They were out again that night, putting up little posters

she'd designed and photocopied, in the shops and on lampposts. 'Missing', and a photo of the dog, then 'Emma – Beloved Pet'. And their phone number, and her mobile number. He went left, she went right. He was home first. He fell asleep on the couch. She was in bed when he went up. She wasn't asleep – he knew – but she didn't move or say anything.

They got a few calls.

—I seen your dog.

—How much is the reward?

—I ate Emma.

Kids mostly, messing. And a couple of weird ones. At three in the morning.

—Hello? Are you Emma's dad?

—Emma's a dog.

—Yes.

He was putting the phone down. He could hear the woman at the other end still talking. He put it back to his ear.

—She asked me to tell you she's fine. She's happy.

—She's a fuckin' dog.

—Yes.

He lay back on the bed and knew he'd be getting up in a minute. Sleep was gone.

—Was that someone about Emma? Mary asked.

—Yeah.

—Another nut?

—Maybe we should take the posters down.

—No.

—Okay. You're right. We'll keep at it.

Then there was the website. She showed it to him – www.missingdogs.ie. She'd opened her own page. The same photo of the dog; the location last seen – a little map, their house filled in red. The dog's personality: 'outgoing'.

—Will people look at this? he asked.

—Yes, they will, she said. —Dog lovers will.

—Grand.

—And there are links to other sites, she said.—All over the world.

Some prick in Hong Kong was staring at the picture of their dog.

He said nothing.

Nothing.

That was the way their life had drifted. They never recovered from the dog. They didn't get another one. He wasn't blaming the dog. Things had been heading that way before the dog. The dog had even saved them for a while, or slowed down the drift. They'd had something new in common for a couple of months, and the excursions to the land behind the airport.

He hadn't opened the gate. He hadn't left it open.

But he'd failed. He could have pretended. Cried a bit, let her console him, take over – he didn't know. It wasn't about the gate. It was about grief. She grieved. He didn't. Simple as that. He should have pretended. It would have been a different kind of honesty. He knew that now. He thought he did.

He'd said they should get a new one. She'd stared at him and walked away. It wasn't a house you could walk away in; she had to walk out. She came back. They had another row, and he walked out. It was his turn. He stayed away for hours. He went to the pictures. He came back.

The walking out stopped. The rows stopped. The talking too; it was a wordless life. They'd drifted. But, actually, they hadn't drifted, and that was another problem. One of them should have gone. They should have looked at each other one night, over the dinner or something, and smiled, and known that enough was enough. But that wise moment had never happened. He hadn't let it. He'd wished for it, but he hadn't let it happen. He hadn't let his eyes sit on hers.

Now she was taking off her new coat.

He didn't know her. Didn't know her hair, didn't know why she'd have wanted a tan in January – didn't really know how it was done. Some sort of a lamp, or a bed. He didn't know.

—Your coat's nice, he said.

Animals

He remembers carrying the water tank into the house, trying to make sure he didn't trip over a step or a child. The boys were tiny. And the girls – the twins – must have been so small he can't even imagine them any more. He can't remember filling the tank or dumping the fish into the water, but he sat cross-legged in front of it while the boys gave each fish a name and the eldest, Ben, wrote them in a list with a fat red marker. There were seven fish, seven names – Goldy, Speckly, Big Eyes, and four others. They taped the list to the side of the tank and by the end of the day there were black lines through three of the names and four fish still alive in the tank. The tank stayed in the room – in fact, George left it there when they moved house two years later, long after the last of the fish had been buried.

The animals always had decent, elaborate burials. Christian, Hindu, Humanist – whatever bits of knowledge and shite the kids brought home from school went into the funerals. George changed mobile phones, not because he really wanted to, but because he knew the boxes would come in handy – it was always wise to have a coffin ready for the next dead bird or fish.

He came home one Saturday morning. He'd been away, in England. The house was empty. Sandra, his wife, had taken the kids to visit her mother in Wexford. George put his bag down, went across to the kettle, and saw the brand-new cage – and the canary. And the note, red marker again: 'Feed it'. And he would have, happily, if the canary hadn't been dead. He had a shower, phoned for a taxi, waited an hour for it to arrive, and told the driver to bring him to Wacker's pet shop in Donaghmede.

—Are yeh serious? said the driver.

—Yeah, said George.

—What's in Wacker's that's so special?

George waited till the driver had started the taxi.

—Pets, he said.

He was pleased with his answer.

—Alright, said the driver.

He went through the gears like he was pulling the heads off orphans.

Wacker – or whoever he was – had no canaries. Neither did the guy beside Woodie's. Or the shop on Parnell Street. When the kids got home the next day they found that the canary had turned into two finches. George explained it to them, although they weren't that curious; two of anything was better than one.

—A fella on the plane told me that finches were much

better than canaries. So I swapped the canary for these lads here. A boy and a girl.

—Cool.

He'd no idea at the time if that was true – the male and the female – but it must have been, because they made themselves a nest, and an egg was laid. But nothing hatched. Sandra bought a book and a bigger cage and better nesting material, and the two finches became three, then five, then back to four, three and two. More funerals, more dead bodies in the garden. They got an even bigger cage, a huge thing on wheels. The finches, Pete and Amy – he knows the names, as solidly as his kids' names – built a nest in the top corner, a beehive of a thing. Amy stayed in there while Pete came out, hung on the bars of the cage and looked intelligent.

George went to his mother's house one day, to change a few lightbulbs and put some old crap up into the attic for her. He made a morning of it, smuggled the book he was reading out of the house, bought a takeaway coffee, drove to the seafront and stayed there for an hour after he'd finished at his mother's, parked facing Europe, reading, until he got to the end of a chapter – *The Mambo Kings Play Songs of Love* – and needed to go for a piss. He drove home and walked into the end of the world. Sandra had decided that the morning needed a project, so herself and the kids had wheeled the cage outside and started to go at it with soapy brushes and cloths. A child opened the hatch, Pete flew out, and George found four hysterical children in the kitchen, long past tears and snot, and a woman outside in the back garden, talking to the hedge.

—I can hear him, she said.

—Where?

—In there, she said.

She was pointing into the hedge, which stretched from the house to the end wall. It was a long garden, a grand hedge.

—I can hear him.

George could hear the kids in the house. He could hear lawnmowers and a couple of dogs and the gobshite three doors up who thought he was Barry White. He couldn't hear Pete. But he did hear – he definitely heard it – the big whoop of a great idea going off in his head.

—Listen, he said.—I'm going to bring the kids to Wacker's, to see if Pete flew back there. Are you with me?

Sandra looked at him. And he knew: she was falling in love with him, all over again. Or maybe for the first time – he didn't care. There was a woman in her dressing gown, looking attractively distraught, and she was staring at George like he was your man from *ER*.

—While I'm doing that, said George,—you phone Wacker's and tell him the story. You with me?

—Brilliant.

—It might work.

—It's genius.

—Ah well.

It did work and it was George's greatest achievement. The happiness he delivered, the legend he planted – his proudest moment.

All of the gang in Wacker's were waiting, pretending to be busy. George carried the girls up to the counter; the boys held onto him.

—Dylan here's finch flew away, said George.—And he was thinking that maybe he flew back here.

The lad behind the counter looked up from the pile of receipts he was wrapping with an elastic band.

—Zebra finch?

Dylan nodded.

—He flew in twenty minutes ago.

—Flaked, he was, said an older man who was piling little bales of straw and hay.—Knackered. Come on over and pick him out, Dylan.

There were thirty finches charging around a cage the size of a bedroom. Dylan was pointing before he got to the cage.

—Him.

—Him?

—Yeah.

The older man opened a small side door and put his hand in. He was holding a net, and had the finch out and in his fist with a speed and grace that seemed rehearsed and brilliant.

—This him?

—Yeah.

—What's his name again?

—Pete.

The new Pete wasn't a patch on the old Pete – he was a bit drugged-looking. George liked the finches but they were a pain in the neck – the shit, the sandpaper, food, water. He was halfway to Galway one day when they had to turn back because they'd forgotten about the birds and who was going to look after them; they couldn't come home – they were going for two weeks – to a stinking kitchen and a cage full of tiny, perfect skeletons. They found a neighbour willing to do the job and started off again, a day late. Sandra told George to stop gnashing his teeth; he hadn't been aware that he'd been doing it. The fuckin' birds. But then, another time, he was up earlier than usual – this was back home. He went into the kitchen and saw Dylan sitting in the dawn light, watching the cage, watching Pete and Amy. George stood there and watched Dylan. Another of those great moments. *This is why I live.*

George is walking the new dog. A Cavalier spaniel. A rescue dog. He looks down at it trotting beside him, and wonders again what *rescue* means. The dog is perfect, but it had to be rescued from its previous owners. He's walking the dog because he likes walking the dog and he has nothing else to do. His kids are reared and he's unemployed. He's getting used to that – to both those facts. The election posters are on every pole, buckled by rain and heat – it's early June and the weather's great.

The guinea pigs stayed a day and a half and introduced the house to asthma. George came home from work – he remembers that feeling – and the boys showed him the Trousers Trick.

—Look, they said, and brought him over to the new cage – another new cage. There were two guinea pigs inside, in under shredded pages of the *Evening Herald*.

Ben, the eldest, opened the cage and grabbed one of the guinea pigs, and George's objections – unsaid, unexplored – immediately broke up and became nothing. The confidence, the sureness of the movement, the hand, the arm into the cage – the kid was going to be a surgeon. He held the guinea pig in both hands.

—What's his name?

—Guinea Pig, said Ben.

He got down on the kitchen floor. Dylan had grabbed the other pig and was down beside his brother.

—Look.

They sat, legs out and apart. It was summer and they were wearing shorts, and that was where the guinea pigs were sent – up one leg of each pair. George watched the guinea pigs struggling up the boys' legs, heard the boys' laughter and screams as they tried to keep their legs straight. Dylan sat up and pulled a leg down, to make room for his guinea pig to bridge the divide and travel down the other leg. It was a joy to watch – and Ben actually became a barman. But that night, he started coughing and wheezing, and scratching his legs till they bled. His eyes went red and much too big for his face. They suddenly had a child with allergies and asthma and the guinea pigs were gone – replaced by the rabbits.

The first dog ate one of the rabbits. George wasn't sure any more if it had been one of the first, original rabbits. He could go now, he could turn and walk to Ben's place of work, the next pub after George's local – a fifteen-minute walk – and ask him. It's early afternoon, and the place will be quiet. He can leave the dog tied to the bike rack outside, have a quick pint or just a coffee – the coffee in a pub with a bike rack is bound to be drinkable. He could do that; he has the time. But he doesn't want to seem desperate, because that's how he feels.

The Lost Decade – that was what the American economist called it, Paul Krugman, the fella who'd won the Nobel Prize, on the telly, a few weeks before. He hadn't been talking about the last decade; it was the next one. It already had a name, and George knew he was fucked.

The quick decision to get rid of the guinea pigs – George hadn't a clue now what had happened to them; something else he could check with Ben – had brought biblical grief down on the house. Ben had actually torn his T-shirt off his own back.

—It's my fault! It's my fault!

—Ah, it's not.

—It is!

They filled the car and headed straight to Wacker's. Did George ever go to work back then? His memory is clogged with cars, years, full of happy and unhappy children. Shouting at traffic lights, trying to distract the kids, getting them to sing along to the Pretenders' Greatest Hits, the Eurythmics' Greatest Hits, the Pogues' Greatest Hits. *We had five million hogs and six million dogs, and seven million barrels of porr-horter.* Sandra held Ben's hand and walked him around the pet shop, looking at his eyes. She kept him well away from the guinea pigs. She bent his head over a bucket of rabbits.

—Breathe.

—Mammy, I am breathing. I have to.

—Let's see you.

George watched Sandra examining Ben's eyes, face. He was keeping the others outside, at the door, so they couldn't gang up on Ben if he failed the test and they had to go home empty-handed. But he could tell, Ben was grand. They'd be bringing home a rabbit.

They brought home three and the dog ate one of them. He didn't *eat* the rabbit, exactly. He perforated the spleen and left it on the back step. The rabbit looked perfect, and even more dead because of that.

Suffer, your man Krugman said, when he was asked how Ireland should deal with the next ten years. Well, this is George, suffering.

Those years, when the mortgage was new and money was scarce, when the country seemed to be taking off, waking up or something, when the future was a long, simple thing, a beach. When he could hold Sandra and tell her they'd be fine, she'd be fine. The first miscarriage, her father's death, his own scare – he'd never doubted that they'd be grand.

He stands outside the pub, away from the windows – he doesn't want Ben looking out and seeing him there. He isn't even sure if Ben is on today, or on the early shift.

Gone. That certainty. It wasn't arrogance. Maybe it was – he doesn't know. It doesn't feel like a sin or a crime. He exploited no one; he invested in nothing. He has one mortgage, one credit card. One mortgage, no job. Seven years left on the mortgage and no prospect of a fuckin' job. He'll be near retirement age by the time they – *he* gets through the lost decade. He'll have nothing to retire from and the dog he's tying to the bike rack will be dead. And there won't be another dog. This one here is the last animal.

The girls found the rabbit on the back step and they went hysterical – everyone went hysterical. No one blamed the dog. It was his instinct, his nature. So George couldn't get rid of him. But then he bit Ben's best friend, and fuck nature; he was gone, down to the vet, put out of George's misery.

—It's for the best.

Goofy was the dog's name. Simon was the friend's. Simon was fine but the dog was a bastard. Refused to be trained. Stared back at George as it cocked its leg against the fridge and pissed on it. A bastard. And George hid it, the fact that their dog was a bad-minded fucker, the fact that maybe his family had created this monster. He got up before the rest of them every morning and mopped the shit and piss off the kitchen floor before they woke, had the place clean and smelling of pine when they came in for their Coco Pops and Alpen. When Goofy took a chunk out of Simon – when George heard about it, when Sandra phoned him at work – as he ran out to the car, he actually felt so relieved that guilt never got a look-in. Two stitches for Simon, death to Goofy. A good bottle of Rioja for Simon's parents.

He didn't have to bury Goofy, or the unfortunate twit that came after him, Simba. George reversed over Simba – heard the yelp, felt the bump – jumped out of the car and, again, felt relief when he saw that it wasn't a child that had gone under the wheel. He looked around; he was on his own. He grabbed Simba's collar and hauled him to the front gate. He looked onto the road, thanked God that he lived in a cul-de-sac, and dragged Simba out to the road. Then he went in and told them the bad news: some bollix had run over Simba. And felt proud of himself as he wiped tears and promised ice cream and prawn crackers. He never told anyone what had actually happened and had never felt a bit of guilt about the cover-up. Although the oul' one across the road looked at him like he was a war criminal and he wondered if she'd been looking out her window when he'd dragged Exhibit A down the drive. But he didn't care that much and, anyway, she was dead now too. There's a gang of Poles renting that house now – or, there was. It's been quiet over there for a while, and he wonders if they've left, moved on. There are stories of cars abandoned in the airport car park; the place is supposed to be stuffed with them.

He pats the dog. She's a tiny little thing, smaller still on a windy day when her fur is beaten back against her.

—Twenty minutes, he says.

He's actually talking to the dog, out on the street. He's losing it.

He straightens up. He looks down at the dog. He can't leave it here. It'll be stolen, the leash will loosen – she'll run out on the street. He can't do it.

He pushes open the pub door. He was right – it's quiet. It's empty. There's no one behind the bar. He waits

– he doesn't step in. He wants to keep an eye on the dog. Then there's a white shirt in the gloom, and he can make out the face. It's Ben, his son.

—Da?

—Ben.

—Are you alright?

—I'm grand. I've the dog outside—

—Bring her in.

—I don't want to get you in trouble.

He shouldn't have said that – it sounds wrong. Like he's trivialising Ben – his job.

—It's cool, says Ben.—I can say it's your guide dog.

He's come out from behind the bar. He's twenty-two but he's still the lanky lad he suddenly became six years ago.

—I'll get her, he says.

He passes George, and comes back quickly holding the dog like a baby.

—She had a crap earlier, George tells him.

—That's good, says Ben.—So did I.

He puts the dog down, ties the leash to one of the tall stool legs.

—You sit there, he says.—So she can't pull it down on herself.

—Grand.

George sits. Then he stands, takes off his jacket – it's too hot for a jacket; he shouldn't have brought it. He sits again.

—Quiet, he says.

—Yeah.

—Is that the recession?

—Not really, says Ben.—It's always quiet this time. What'll yeh have?

—What's the coffee like?

—Don't do it.

—No coffee?

—No. Nothing that needs a kettle.

—I'll chance a pint.

He watches Ben putting the glass under the tap, holding the glass at the right angle. He's never seen him at work before, and knows that he'd be just as relaxed if the place was packed, the air full of shouts for drink.

—Everything okay, Da?

—Grand, yeah. Not a bother.

—How's Ma?

—Grand, says George.—Great. Remember the rabbits?

—The rabbits?

—The hutch. Goofy killed one of them. Remember?

—Yeah.

He puts the glass back under the tap. He tops up the pint. He pushes a beer mat in front of George. He puts the pint on top of it.

—Lovely.

George gets a tenner out of his pocket, hands it out to Ben.

—There you go.

Ben takes it. He turns round to the till, opens it, takes out George's change. He puts it beside George's pint.

—Thanks, says George.—There were three rabbits, am I right?

—Yeah, says Ben.—Not for long, but.

—What were they called?

—Liza, Breezy and Doughnut.

—And Goofy ate Breezy.

—Liza, says Ben.—Why?

—Nothing, really, says George.—Nothing important. It just came into my head.

The pint's ready. He hasn't had a pint in a good while. He tastes it.

—Grand.

—Good.

—Good pint.

—Thanks.

—Do you like the work?

—It's alright, says Ben.—Yeah. Yeah, I like it.

—Good, says George.—That's good.

He hears the door open behind him. He looks down at the dog. She stays still.

—Good dog.

Ben goes down the bar, to meet whoever's just come in.

George loves the dog. Absolutely loves it. She's a Cavalier. A King Charles spaniel, white and brown. George loves picking her up, putting her on his shoulder. He knows what he's at, making her one of the kids. But she's only a dog and she's doomed. George watched a documentary on Sky: *Bred to Die*. About pedigree dogs. And there was one of his, a Cavalier, sitting on the lap of a good-looking woman in a white coat, a vet or a scientist. And she starts explaining that the dog's brain is too big —*It's like a size 10 foot shoved into a size 6 shoe*. The breeders have been playing God, mating fathers and mothers to their sons and daughters, siblings to siblings, just so they'll look good – *consistent* – in the shows. Pugs' eyes fall out of their heads, bulldogs can no longer mate, Pekinese have lungs that wouldn't keep a fly in the air. And his dog has a brain that's being shoved out of her head, down onto her spine.

He leans down, picks up the dog. He can do it one-handed; she's close to weightless.

Ben is back at the taps. Pulling a pint of Heineken for the chap at the other end of the bar.

The dog on George's lap is a time bomb.

She's going to start squealing, whimpering, some day. And that'll be that.

He won't get another one.

—Remember Simba?

Ben looks up from the glass.

—I do, yeah. Why?

—I hit him, says George.

—You never hit the dogs, Da.

Ben looks worried.

—No, says George.—With the car.

—With the car?

—I reversed over him.

—Why?

—Not on purpose, says George.—I was just parking.

Fair play to Ben, he fills the glass, brings it down to the punter, takes the money, does the lot without rushing or staring at George.

He's back.

—Why didn't you tell us?

—Well, says George.—I don't really know. Once I saw it wasn't one of you I'd hit, I didn't give much of a shite. And the chance was there, to drag him out to the road. And once I'd done that, I couldn't drag him back – you know.

—Why now?

—Why tell you?

—Yeah.

—I don't know. I was just thinking about it – I don't know.

—It doesn't matter.

—I know, says George.—But it would have, then. When you were all small.

—No, says Ben.—It would've been alright.

—Do you reckon?

Ben looks down the bar.

—Listen, he says.—We all knew we had a great da.

George can't say anything.

His heart is too big for him, like the dog's brain. The blood's rushing up to his eyes and his mouth. Him and the dog, they'll both explode together.

Bullfighting

He couldn't really remember life before the children. He couldn't feel it as something he'd once lived. It was too far away, and buried. Something as simple as walking down the street – he was always a father. Or looking at a woman – he was a father.

He had one child left. There'd been four, but three of them were up and running, more or less their own men. They were all boys, still teenagers. But they weren't his any more. Except for the youngest. That was Peter. Peter still held Donal's hand. Except when there were people coming towards them, boys or girls his own age or older. Then he'd let go, until they were around the corner.

And Donal knew. One day soon he'd open his hand for Peter's, and it would stay empty. And when that happened he'd die; he'd lie down on the ground. That was how he felt. After twenty years. Independence, time to himself – he didn't want it.

—You'll have your own life, someone had told him.

—I have my own life, he'd said back.—I fuckin' like it.

He'd never felt hard done by – he didn't think he had. He'd loved the life, even the stress of it. He'd be knackered tired sometimes, red-eyed and soggy, only vaguely aware that he had a name or even a gender, and still he'd think, *I'm alive*. Making a dinner he knew none of them would eat, or charging in to Temple Street Hospital with a wheezing or a bleeding child, or standing at the side of a football pitch, in the pissing rain, twenty miles from home, watching one of the boys trying to make sure that the ball didn't go anywhere near him. The boys had been the rhythm of every day, even when he was sleeping. He woke before they did, always. None of his lads had ever walked into an empty kitchen first thing in the morning.

There was once, he was changing a nappy. Carl's – Carl was the second. They were at Elaine's mother's place. It was a Sunday afternoon. He had Carl parked in front of him, on the edge of his changing mat, his arse in the air, right over Elaine's ma's white carpet. He pulled the nappy out from under Carl and the shite jumped free of the nappy, a half-solid ball. Without thinking, Donal caught it – his hand just went out. The nappy in one hand, the shite in the other, Carl's arse hanging over the carpet. And he couldn't wait to tell everyone. He knew he had his story.

The stories – twenty years of them.

They already seemed stale. They'd been over-lived, dragged out too often. He'd start talking, even thinking, and he'd feel the camera lights, the heat. He'd imagine he was talking to a studio audience, selling something, trying to convince them. But there was nothing dishonest about how he felt. Empty. Finished. The stories, his memories, were wearing out and there was nothing new replacing them. His whole fuckin' life was going.

He watched telly now with Peter. A film on Sky Movies. *Little Man*. It was dreadful. This tiny little black guy was pretending he was a baby – Donal didn't know why; they'd missed the start – staring at a woman's tits, trying to grab at them. It was absolutely dreadful. But Peter was laughing, so he did too.

—Should we be even watching this, Pete?

—It's appropriate, said Peter.—I checked.

—But he wants to have sex with the woman.

—So do you, said Peter.

—Okay, said Donal.—Fair enough.

One last story for the file: *So do you, he says.*

Peter was ten. Donal was forty-eight. So were his friends. He liked the precision of that: all his friends were forty-eight. It was the best thing about Ireland, about Dublin anyway; he could still see the men he'd grown up with. He'd gone to school with lads who'd moved to Canada, the States, even South Africa. But no one he knew had ever moved south of the Liffey. They'd either got out of the country or stayed put. And Donal had been lucky. He'd walked out of school in 1977, and straight into a job in the civil service. A few years later, the jobs weren't there. But Donal had never been out of work. And his friends were like him. They lived in houses a few miles from where they'd all grown up.

They could walk to the pub. It wasn't the same place where they'd had their first pints, but that place was only two miles away.

They met up once a week. All four of them, or three of them, or even just the two. It was an open kind of arrangement, but a bit more organised since they'd started the texting a few years back. *Pub? Ye. 9.30? Grnd.* Donal never felt tired on Thursday nights. He'd be away on holidays – in France, say, or Portugal, or Orlando, in the States – having a great time. But on the Thursday, wherever, he wished he was at home, on his way up to the pub.

It had always been like that. There was once, early on with Elaine, they'd been on the bed, in his flat. She'd just poured a melted Mars bar into her navel. And she caught him looking at his watch.

—Have you something more important to do?

—God, no. Fuck, no. This is brilliant.

The hot chocolate had burnt his tongue a bit and he'd felt a little bit sick. But it had been great. He could still remember her stomach under his tongue.

—This is the first thing I've eaten since me breakfast, he told her, and she laughed and he could feel that too, rippling her skin, lifting her. He'd held her – he told her this years later – he'd held her hips to keep her on her back, so that none of the melted chocolate would drop onto the sheet, because it was the only sheet he had and he didn't want her to know that. He ate the chocolate, cleaned it all up, and then he didn't care what way she ended up. It was up to her.

His friends never talked about sex, or health. They never had. Or problems – they didn't really talk about their problems.

Other people didn't really get it. Especially women. Grown men getting together like that, as if it was weird or unnatural. Or a bit silly.

—Are you meeting the lads tonight?

—I'm not answering, if you're going to sneer like that.

—Like what?

—The *lads*.

She'd even asked him once, when he was putting his shoes on.

—What use are they?

—What?

—The lads, she'd said.—Your friends.

—What about them?

—Why are they your friends?

—I'm not answering that.

—Don't be so touchy, she said.—I'm curious.

—Well, stay curious.

—I'm sorry. I didn't mean anything.

—Why do I have to defend myself?

—You don't.

—I have to explain why my friends are my friends. Why the fuck should I?

—Don't, if you don't want to.

—I never ask you about your friends, he said.

—I *know*, she said.—You don't even know their names.

—I do.

She smiled.

—I *do*, he insisted.—There's Mary and—

—Stop, she said.—Listen. I suppose what I'm wondering is. What do you talk about?

He looked at her.

—Football, he said.

He knew she'd hate the answer.

—Is that all?

—No.

—What else? she said.—Help me here.

He didn't know what else to give her. He didn't know how to explain it. How what they talked about wasn't important. How they could sit and say nothing much, for most of the night. And he'd still come home feeling great.

Appreciated.

—Jokes, he said.

—You tell jokes.

—Yeah, he said.—If we've heard any new ones.

—That's nice.

She wasn't sneering.

—Mind you, he said.—You never hear jokes these days. It's all e-mail stuff. No one makes up jokes any more. Like stories, you know.

She nodded.

—Can I go now? he said.

—Go on.

He smiled. She smiled back.

He was the first in. Their usual table was free. He nodded at the barman, raised one finger. He always liked that.

The fact that he could order a pint without talking. He'd been coming here for years. The barman was Polish. He'd only been working here for three months or so, but he knew what Donal's order was, and Donal had never had to tell him. The Poles were great.

He sat and looked at the snooker on the telly. He hadn't a clue who was playing. He didn't know either of the players. They looked younger than his older kids. Hair gel, and little rectangular ads stitched onto their waistcoats. They looked too young to be out in the world on their own, millionaires already, more than likely.

He was out of touch. He knew it.

The lounge girl came up with his pint in the centre of her tray.

—Thanks, said Donal.

—Of course.

She was Lithuanian, as far as Donal remembered. Or Latvian. A lovely young one, lovely attitude.

He gave her a tenner. She gave him his change, and he gave her back some of it.

—Thank you.

—You're grand.

Donal felt the draught, and saw Gerry closing the door behind him.

The lounge girl was waiting.

—Will you like another pint of Guinness?

—Great, yeah. Thanks.

He felt a bit uncomfortable with her. She was a woman and a girl – that was the problem. And the attraction.

And the problem. He'd have been happier with a lounge boy.

—Fuckin' cold out there, said Gerry.

This was how it happened. They arrived in a clump, from one man to four inside a minute or two. As if they'd been hiding behind the bushes outside until one of them made the move and went in. Or something, an instinct, told the four of them to get up from the telly and go, at the same time every Thursday.

Donal watched the other two, Ken and Seán, wrap the wires around their iPods and put them into their jacket pockets. He decided again; he'd get an iPod.

—What were yis listening to? he asked.

—Springsteen, said Ken.

—The new album?

—Yep.

—Any good?

—His best since the last one.

The young one brought the pints. Donal paid her, and tipped her again. He'd given her €4, for one round. It made him feel seedy, and generous.

They'd have four pints. They might go to five. Four was automatic. The fifth was always a decision. It used to be more. They used to drink all day, days in a row, weekends drunk, into work on Monday, drunk. Donal and Gerry had gone twenty-four hours once, in Majorca. They'd found a bar that would let them drink till daylight. They'd had breakfast – Traditional English Breakfast – on the way back to the apartment. He remembered being surprised that he could hold the knife and fork.

Seán looked around.

—How many in here would you say have snorted cocaine?

—None, said Gerry.

He was probably right.

—Not according to the news, said Seán.—We're all fuckin' snorting.

—I've never even seen cocaine, said Gerry.—Have any of youse?

They shook their heads.

Some young one, a model, had died, and two other kids in Wexford or Waterford – they'd eaten damp cocaine. The radio was full of it, and the television. Middle-class men, their faces fuzzy and their voices disguised, describing their cocaine hells. 'It's on the cheeseboard. Every dinner party I've been to.' And hidden cameras, in pub toilets. More fuzzy faces, leaning over cisterns, with rolled-up euros.

—What about your kids? said Ken.

They all had kids, teenagers and older.

Donal shrugged.

—Don't know, he said.—Don't think so.

—How do you know?

—I don't, said Donal.—But I think I would.

Gerry nodded.

—How would we know? he said.—Unless they went crazy, or something.

—A swab, said Seán.

—What?

—A swab. Of the cistern, or a shelf. For traces of cocaine.

They laughed. Three of them laughed.

—You couldn't do that in my house, said Gerry.—The jacks is never empty.

—I did, said Seán.

They looked at him. They stared at him.

—You did a – what? – a test? A fuckin' swab?

—Yep, said Seán.

—Did you get a kit or something? Gerry asked him.—Do you not have to be a fuckin' forensics expert or something?

—Not at all, said Seán.—All you need is a cotton bud. I ran one across the top of the jacks. The cistern, like.

—And?

—It was filthy.

They laughed again.

—White particles, said Seán.

—Dust, said Donal.—Talc. The jacks would be full of it. Any room. The air's full of dust.

—Did you have them tested? The white particles.

—No, said Seán.

—So? said Gerry.—What did you prove?

—I sniffed the bud, said Seán.—Snorted it, like. So to speak.

—And?

—I was high as a fuckin' kite.

He was joking.

—Dancing with the fridge. Seriously though, he said.—I've been watching my girls since it got into the news. And they're the same as they've ever been. So they either aren't using cocaine or they've always been using cocaine.

He shrugged.

—They're grand, he said.—The only one that might be snorting is Maeve.

Maeve was his wife.

—D'you reckon?

—It would explain quite a lot, said Seán.

He left it at that. They didn't talk about the wives. They drifted from cocaine to football, and on to the film that Gerry had seen at the weekend and the others wanted to see.

—How was Denzel?

—Brilliant.

And on to international affairs.

—Poor oul' Benazir.

—What a place.

—Mad. Would you have given her one?

—Oh, yeah. Absolutely.

—Too late now, an'anyway.

—She was a fine thing. I liked her headscarf.

—That's the thing though, said Donal.—Women don't wear them here any more.

—Not even at mass.

—They'll make a comeback, said Ken.—Wait and see. Abercrombie and Fitch or somebody will bring back the headscarf.

—Benazir but, said Gerry. —She was a lot better looking than any of the women politicians in this country.

—That's for sure.

—What about Hillary Clinton?

—No.

—A few years back, maybe. Not now, though.

—She'd be saying the same thing about us.

—She hasn't a clue.

—Would you ride Obama?

—Not unless he was a woman.

—I have a dream.

That was the same night the idea was planted. They'd go away together, to Spain.

—The four of us?

—Why not? said Gerry.

—Sounds good.

Gerry's brother had a place down there.

—Where?

—Valencia. Near there. A half-hour or so. Inland. No sand or shite. It's great.

There was no decision that night, nothing firm. Donal said nothing to Elaine about it. He waited for Gerry to bring it up the next Thursday.

—Did yis give any more thought to that?

—What? said Ken.

—Spain.

—Your brother's gaff?

—Yeah.

They looked at one another, and shrugged, and smiled.

—Well, I'm going, said Gerry.

—Grand.

* * *

They went a few weeks after Easter. A Ryanair flight to Valencia, then a hired car. Donal had driven in France, but in his own car; they'd always got the ferry. They'd been to France four times. Always the same place, camping. The last time was five years ago. The year after that, the eldest, Matthew, said he wouldn't go. They couldn't make him – he was fifteen – and he was too young to leave behind.

They drove into the town. It seemed deserted, and a bit ugly.

—Is this the siesta?

—Suppose so.

It was early afternoon.

Gerry parked outside a bar.

—There's people in there, so they're not all asleep.

They sat outside, with four bottles of beer that cost the same as one bottle at home. Seán took off his jumper.

—That's it, lads. I'm on me holidays.

—Good man.

—How far is the house?

—Three minutes.

—Grand.

—This is fuckin' great, said Donal.

But he was disappointed. It *was* great, a week away from everything. But the town itself was shite. It was dead. Their table was on a street, but it didn't matter because the street was empty. He sat up and looked properly.

—What's that?

—What?

—The wall down there. The curved wall.

—The bullring, said Gerry.

—For bullfighting?

—Yeah.

—Serious?

—Yeah.

—Great.

—No, said Gerry.—It's a pain in the hole. Boring.

—Still, though, said Donal.

—Do they kill the bulls?

—Yeah.

—Cool.

—They, like, release them first, said Gerry.—Let them run through the streets.

—And that's fuckin' boring, is it? said Seán.

—It is, said Gerry.—Believe me.

—Still though, said Donal.

—It's the fiesta, said Gerry.—The annual festival. Saint something. Or the Virgin Mary.

—They slaughter bulls for the Virgin Mary?

—Wait'll you see it later, said Gerry.—It's good. The fiesta bit. He stood up.

They got back in the car. Gerry took them out of the town, past a field full of solar panels, and behind a small industrial estate. In Dublin, this was where you would dump the body or the fridge. Here it was a row of flat-roofed houses, under palm trees.

—Here we are.

It was the last house in the row.

Gerry got out and unlocked the gate. They got out and followed him. They saw the pool but kept behind

Gerry as he got the front door open and walked into hot dead air.

—Fuckin' hell.

They hoisted the shutters and opened all the windows. There weren't many; it wasn't a big house. They threw bags on the beds and then they went out to the pool.

—It's nice and clean.

—There's a chap keeps an eye on it for Declan.

Declan was Gerry's brother.

—He throws in the chlorine and scoops out the flies and that.

—What's that?

There was a white machine, like a fat pup with a trunk, moving very slowly along the bottom.

—It's a hoover, said Gerry.

—For fuck sake. Is it on all the time?

—Think so, yeah.

—Clever.

—It's useless, said Gerry.—If it's the same one. It just moves into a corner and stays there. So the corner's spotless and the rest of it gets covered in fuckin' goo.

They got into the togs and sat looking at the water and, one at a time, they got in because there wasn't really room for more than one man, the way they swam. They sat with their backs to the industrial estate and let themselves get hungry. They chatted and kept an eye on the sun. The watches were off, thrown onto the beds. They had one more swim, then showered and put on the shorts and T-shirts. The shorts were new. They never wore shorts at home.

—Is that a bruise?

—Varicose vein.

—Lovely.

—You can show it to whatever young one you pick up tonight in town.

—I'll tell yeh. Show a bird your varicose veins and she'll be on you like a fuckin' barnacle.

They waited till Gerry locked the gate.

—Dogs, he said.—Have to keep them out.

—What? said Donal.—Wild?

—Kind of.

—Jaysis.

—It's the one bad thing, said Gerry.—The way they treat the dogs.

And now they could hear them. Dogs howling, baying – whatever it was.

—Are they all wild?

—No, said Gerry. —Just fuckin' miserable.

Gerry showed them the lane that would get them to town. They walked, all four men in a row. The sandals slapped the dust.

They went past the industrial estate and the tied-up dogs.

—What gets made in there?

—Nothing. As far as I know.

—Distribution?

—Maybe. But I've never seen a truck.

—Who feeds the dogs?

—There's an automatic feeder. It releases enough food every day. And water. They all have them. Most of the houses are empty during the week.

—That's terrible.

—Talkin' about feeders, said Donal,—I'm fuckin' starving.

They all were.

—A few scoops, a game of pool and the nosebag. How's that for a plan?

They ignored the bullfighting. It was on the telly, a local channel, in the bar. And it was outside. There were people running down the street, and back up the street. And a marching band, somewhere. Donal wanted to have a look, but Gerry was the local and he didn't even look out the window. And, fair enough, it all looked shite on the telly. There was a bull standing still, outside a church – it looked like. And young lads, all young lads, were walking carefully up to it, and touching it and dashing back. It looked like something anyone could do. The young lads all wore red T-shirts. Trying to provoke the bull, he supposed. But the bull wasn't having any of it. He just stood there, still. Then he was gone, off the screen, in the time it took Donal to bend down at the table and pretend he was sizing up his shot – he hadn't a clue, really. The commentator was going mad but all Donal could see was the door of the church.

They finished the game and went walking. The excitement was still in the street. The young lads, bashing against one another, thumping their chests. There was no sign of the bull, although there was dung in the air and – Donal saw it now – blood on the street. A topic for the phone call home in the morning. The marching band was still marching, but they still hadn't seen it. There were stalls down both sides of the main street, and Donal saw some of the stuff he'd bring home, the small presents the kids used to charge down the hall for when they heard him coming in the door, after he'd been away for a day or two because of work.

They found a place and ate well. Good, big steaks.

—Straight off the fuckin' bull.

The waiter recognised Gerry, smiled at him.

—Irish, yes?

—Yeah; good man.

—How are you? said the waiter.

—Good, said Gerry.—Yeah. How's business?

—You are my business.

He clapped his hands.

—Business is good.

They stopped at another bar. Another few drinks, at a table outside. The loud young lads were gone. There were families strolling, proud men pushing buggies.

—It's after one.

—A different world.

—It's very civilised.

—If this was Dublin, we'd be watching the fight.

—We'd be at home.

They walked back to the house at about three.

—A swim?

—Don't be fuckin' stupid.

They slept through the dogs. The room was still dark when Donal woke. But there was a day outside; he could feel it pressing against the shutter. He got out of the bed, and he was grand. No bother. He went out to the hall and looked at his phone. One o'clock. He'd woken up in the afternoon. He couldn't remember the last time that had happened. Long before kids, before marriage. He went out to the pool, and Gerry was there, listening to his iPod.

Donal sat beside him.

—What're you listening to?

—The Cure.

—The Cure? Are they still good?

—They're great. Hang on. I can link this up to the speakers inside. It'll wake the other pair up.

He went inside and, a minute later, Donal was listening to 'The Love Cats'. Gerry came back with a pot of good, solid coffee. The other two got up. They chatted. They swam. They read. They ate some bread and cheese. They got bored with the Cure, so Gerry changed it to Echo and the Bunnymen. Donal was definitely getting an iPod. He'd forgotten these bands had existed.

—D'you remember Japan?

—They haven't aged well.

—Have they not? What about Madness?

—Kids love Madness.

—*I* love Madness. Talking Heads?

—They're next.

The sun started dipping, and Seán came out with four bottles of Stella.

That was their week in Spain. Their routine. Like

heaven, in the Talking Heads song. Where nothing ever happened.

The songs were queuing up.

He rang home every day, walked around the pool while he talked to Elaine and Peter, and the older boys if they were at home. He texted them too. *Hw'r things?* They usually got back to him. *Gnd*, or *Gud*, or *Fin. U?* But he didn't really miss them. He didn't think about them. He didn't ache to hold them as they used to be, their weight in his arms, their smells under his nose. He didn't mind being alone in the bed, when he woke. He liked it, just himself, nothing to remember or catch up on. He stopped hearing the dogs.

The three lads were up before him one of the mornings. Gerry was walking around the pool, worrying the hoover with the butt of a brush, pushing it out towards the centre. Ken had his BlackBerry, was poking away at it with the little plastic stick.

He put it on the table.

—There now, he said. —That should keep the economy afloat.

—Day's work done?

—And no one even knows I'm here. This is the world we live in, men.

Ken had rigged his life so that where he actually was rarely mattered. And Gerry was the same. Gerry and Ken had slid into self-employment, about fifteen years before. Donal hadn't noticed – too busy changing nappies. And he was happy enough where he was, in the Revenue. He still liked it, going after the farmers. He'd found bogus accounts and all sorts of hidden accounts. Hairy men with shite on their boots, with millions stashed away in the Caymans and Bermuda, or in biscuit tins under their beds. A few years back, he'd been asked into an office, for a chat. Had he ever thought of the CAB? He must have looked a bit slack-jawed, because the man in a better suit than Donal's added a word to each of the letters.

—Criminal Assets Bureau. Would you be up for it?

—Are they not the Guards? said Donal.—Cops. Going after gangsters?

—It's liquid, said his boss's boss.—You'd be on secondment. And, now, you wouldn't be breaking down doors or anything like that. It wouldn't be *The Untouchables*. Will you think about it, anyway? We wouldn't be asking if we didn't think you were the man they needed.

—Thanks.

—You'll think about it?

—Yeah, he said.—I will.

—I'll leave it with you.

He didn't tell Elaine; he told no one. He was flattered, thrilled. He actually saw himself in the part; he felt the door give way against his shoulder. Felt the weight of the shotgun. Felt – saw – his eyes match the look coming at him from the drugs baron across the room.

They never came back to him about it, but that didn't matter. He couldn't have gone to work knowing that

Elaine or the kids were worried about him. He didn't think it was just an excuse, or a lie. He didn't think it then – he wasn't sure. It was six or seven years ago. Six. And, actually, he *was* sure. He'd wanted nothing to do with gangland warlords or major drug dealers. He was happier with the farmers.

Gerry had always been a bit more daring, or mad. Donal could see him now. He rolled – he multitasked. He scooped the dead stuff out of the pool with a net while he sold a guy in Dublin an insurance policy, or something. An update, Gerry called it.

—You're what? said Gerry, to the phone.—Fifty-two?

Now he was shoving the hoover back to the middle of the pool.

—It's not about the years you've left, Mick, he said.

He was wearing a Red Hot Chili Peppers T-shirt, nearly faded to nothing. One of his kid's, Donal guessed.

—It's about the years you've already lived, he said.— What you have to show for them, what there is to protect. Are you with me?

He sat down and picked up one of the bottles.

—It's not going to get cheaper because you've less years to live. It's insurance I'm selling, not milk. And look, I'm not even selling it. You're already well covered. I'm just telling you about it. I have to. It's the law.

He took a swig from the bottle.

—Spain, he said.—Yeah, it's great. Just me and a few lads. No. No golf. Fuck golf. You know about me and golf. So, anyway, grand, there's no hurry. You phone me, Mick. Either way, yeah. I will, yeah. Good luck.

He put the phone on the table. He said nothing. It was just work, the way he did it now, what he used to do at a desk, or in a pub or a restaurant, five years ago. He'd adjusted. He could work beside a swimming pool in Spain, with his best friends.

—The world, said Ken, one of the nights they were out.

—What about it?

—It's grand, said Ken.—But I worry a bit sometimes.

—Why?

—Not about global warming or that, said Ken.— That'll sort itself out. There'll be good and bad there.

They nodded. They all kind of agreed, and none of them wanted to talk about global warming. They were wearing shorts and sandals. It was boring.

—Just, said Ken.—The future. Like, I've complete faith in us. Our age group. And the very young. Kids, like.

Donal knew what he meant.

—It's the ones in between, he said.

And Ken nodded.

—Exactly, he said.—D'you know many people in their thirties?

—One or two, said Seán.

—Fuckin' eejits, said Ken.—Every one of them. I'm right, amn't I?

—Yeah, said Donal.—But you're right about kids as well. They're brilliant.

They were talking shite, enjoying themselves. But, still and all, Donal nearly cried. He was talking about his own kids. Moving away from him, setting off on their

196

own. He loved it and hated it. He'd never get over it. But he'd have to.

Gerry looked at him.

—Are you alright? he said, quietly.

—I'm grand, said Donal.

And he was. They'd never talk about it. Except agree, and move on.

The day before they went home, they went into Valencia. They got up in time to catch the bus. Past half-built apartment blocks and wasteland – no real countryside, and no sea. They yawned and chatted till Gerry stood up, and they followed him off the bus. They wandered around for a couple of hours. They went into the cathedral. Donal put fifty cent in a slot and watched the electric candles come on. He walked away before they went off again. They went to an old market, the *plaça redonda*, and decided not to buy any bootleg DVDs because they didn't want to carry them around all day and lose them. They went into a tapas place and ate about fifty euros' worth of the little things along the counter. They went to a bar with a big screen, to watch the English football. They had their first beers, slowly, and a few more, slowly, till the match was over, and they went for a stroll. They found a small corner bar with a very good-looking waitress, and they stayed there till it was dark. They talked more than they had all week. Got pissed slowly, enjoyed the fact that they knew they were getting pissed. They couldn't come back from the jacks without slapping a back. The talk got a bit mad. The first ride, the best ride, the weirdest, the longest.

—Four minutes.

—Four and a half.

—Good man.

Ever with another man.

—No.

—No way.

Ever curious.

—No. Not really.

Ever with a relation.

—Does it have to be a blood relation?

—Yeah.

—Then no.

—Who, but?

—Her ma.

—Your mother-in-law?

—Yeah.

—You're jesting.

—I'm not.

—You are.

—Yeah. I am. But it was touch and go. At her da's funeral, you know. Back at the house.

They were the only ones laughing in the bar. They left, and moved on to another one. David Bowie and another good-looking waitress. Donal told them about the job in the CAB. They told him he'd been right not to take it. They all told him that. They had more tapas in another place. Seán told Donal that his marriage was on the rocks. Gerry told Donal that his marriage was on the rocks. Donal told Gerry that his own had been rocky for a while, but that things were grand now, much better. Then he told Seán. And Ken. Then they were in a taxi, heading back to the town. Laughing. Three of them squashed into the back. Gerry in the front beside the driver.

It was three in the morning. There was still a bar open, the one just down from the bullring. Ken went in, came back out with four bottles. They sat. They heard the marching band. It might have been a different band. They still hadn't seen it.

—At this time? said Seán.

—The town that never sleeps.

Donal stood up. He left his bottle on the table. He'd had enough. He wanted the bed.

He walked.

There was some sort of action going on at the bull-ring. The exit gates were open. It was lit, inside. He could see people, lots of young lads, standing in the ring. There was a barrier between him and the ring, like the metal bars of a jail. The bars were wide enough apart for people to get through, but – he supposed – solid enough to stop a bull. He went in, sideways, between two of the bars. He walked onto the ring. It was quiet – he couldn't hear the band – but the seats all around seemed full. A double gate at the other side was wide open, but he couldn't see anything beyond it. The young lads were just standing there.

He heard an engine. A truck, a big one, reversed slowly through the double gates. Lads got out of the way. A man in a black T-shirt jumped out of the cab and went to the back of the truck. There was another man there with him. They lowered the tailgate – Donal heard chains and a rumble – and they stood back. The crowd roared, and he saw the bull charge down the ramp, then stop. Dead still. Like the bull on a wine bottle. Black and huge, and still. The young lads didn't move any nearer, but no one ran. Donal moved a step closer. The truck was leaving, slowly. He watched till it was gone, and the double gates were shut behind it. The bull had moved. Not much – he didn't think – the angle was different, turned more towards Donal. Then the strange thing happened. A man with a burning torch – Donal hadn't seen him arrive – walked right up to the bull and set fire to it. The two horns were on fire. Red flames roared over its head.

There was a hand on Donal's shoulder.

—You might want to step back a bit.

It was Gerry.

—Yeah, said Donal.

—Behind the barrier.

—Yeah.

He looked behind him. He'd gone further than he'd thought – he hadn't thought at all. He was turning away when the bull moved.

—Fuckin' Jesus.

It ran, dashed, in a broken stop–start – fast. Every move covered distance. They wouldn't have had a hope. But it didn't come at them. It went across the ring, then away and out a different gate that Donal hadn't seen.

The horns three times higher, because of the flames. It was gone just as Donal realised he was falling. His chest hit the ground, his chin. He felt grit in his hands. But he was fine, standing up again, grand. He felt his chin. The ring was empty.

—Where's he gone?

There was no blood in his mouth. He rubbed his hands clean.

—That was great, said Donal.—Fuckin' great.

What he'd just seen. What he'd just done.

—I didn't know they set fire to the poor fuckers as well, said Seán.

—Why do they?

—Fuck knows, said Gerry.—It's mad.

They walked to the house. One more beer, out at the pool. Gerry stuck on the music. Donal held the bottle against his chin.

The way the bull had stood absolutely still.

He put the bottle on the table.

Then the movement. Across the ring. The speed. The flames.

He went over to the pool.

The feeling he'd had, before the bull moved. Not caring. But knowing he was safe – it hadn't felt stupid.

He puked into the pool. On his knees. Straight in.

Echo and the Bunnymen. The dogs howling.

There was no more. He lay down. He could hear the hoover under the water.

Gerry was beside him.

—Feeling better?

—Sorry.

—No bother.

—How do you get vomit out of water?

—Don't worry about it. We'll throw in a bucket of chlorine. That should fix it. It'll eat it or something.

Gerry was sitting beside him.

—Alright?

—Grand, said Donal.—Thanks.

—No bother.

—A great day, said Donal.—Wasn't it?

—Yeah, said Gerry.—Brilliant.

—Brilliant.

He lay there for a while longer, his face on his arm. He felt good – clear. He'd get up in a minute. He might finish the bottle. He was fine.

—Fuckin' brilliant.

This was living, he thought. This was happiness.

Sleep

I t was the thing he'd always loved about her. The way she could sleep. Even when they'd just started going with each other, before they really knew each other, he'd lie awake, hoping she'd wake up, praying for it, dying. But even then he'd loved to look at her while she slept. There was something about it that made him feel lucky, or privileged. Or trusted. She could do that beside him, turn everything off, all the defences, and let him watch her.

It wasn't just the drink that knocked Tara out. They drank a lot in the early days. They'd get drunk and braver two nights a week, Fridays and Saturdays. There'd be a taxi or the last bus home, to his flat or hers. Hers was nicer. Tom's flat was a kip, and the bed sagged badly in the middle. They'd paw at each other in the taxi. There was once, a mad night, she took the belt off his trousers, and put it around her neck and pulled. The driver swerved off the road, up onto the path, and stopped.

—Out.

—Ah, come on, she said. She gave him her accent and smile.—We were joking.

—Out, the driver said to the mirror.—Now, or I'll drive yis to the cop shop. It's only around the corner.

Her flat was around the corner too, so they got out and walked the rest of the way. Holding each other, trying to walk side by side. The belt wasn't around her neck and it wasn't around his waist.

—We left it in the fucking taxi.

She pronounced her 'g's. All of them. She was the only person he knew who did that. It still made him weak. Even when she was telling him he was fucking useless. There was one night – it might have been the same night; there were a lot of new, weird nights then – she fell asleep on Friday and woke up on Sunday morning. He was awake on Saturday, as usual. Alert, alive, gasping for water and sex, but content enough with the water. He got out of the bed and went to the kitchen. She had a kitchen, and a jacks. He didn't, not then. His flat was just the one room, and it wasn't big. He had a bed, a table, two chairs, a Baby Belling cooker, and a fridge so small it could only take a salad cream bottle if he sat it on its side. He shared the toilet and bath with three other bedsits, which was fine some times and fuckin' desperate other times.

He went to the kitchen and let the cold tap run. He could remember water bouncing off the bottom of the sink onto his stomach and chest. He couldn't find a glass, so he'd used a mug with blue and white stripes and tea stains inside it. He'd filled it twice and knocked it back. Then he'd filled the mug again and brought it back to the bedroom. He'd got under the duvet, hoping his movements would wake her. He'd yawned, extravagantly – he remembered this. Stretched, extravagantly. His knuckles scraped the wall behind him. The water sloshed around inside him – he felt it, he heard it – then settled.

She wasn't going to wake up. He'd accepted that, and he'd read for a while. *A Tale of Two Cities*. He'd dozed off. He'd read some more – he'd finished the book that day. He'd gone out to the shop and bought rashers and bread, and the *Irish Times* and a packet of Ritchie's Silvermints. He'd made himself a rasher sandwich. He'd left the kitchen door open and the window shut, and hoped the smell would wake her – she loved her grub. But it didn't. He took the rashers back to the bed, and ate and read the paper. Every bit of it. Even the deaths and births and *Presbyterian Notes*. And dozed, and woke and stretched – extravagantly. He got up and went to the jacks and came back, and watched her sleep. It got dark outside, and he put on his clothes and went for a pint in the pub at the top of her road. It was a middle-class place, full of people who looked as if they disapproved of pubs. He was the only man in the place drinking Guinness. This was back in the early eighties, so it was weird. But he'd loved her for that too, the feeling that she was bringing him into a new world. He went back to the flat and stopped for chips on the way. The chipper was posh too: scampi on the menu on the wall behind the counter. He didn't really know what scampi was. He bought himself chips and a spice burger.

He had her keys with him. He let himself in and slammed the door, slightly. He brought the portable telly to the bedroom, got undressed and back under the duvet, and ate the chips and watched *Match of the Day* and a film he couldn't remember now. He turned off the telly and stretched and yawned, and started another book. *Crime and Punishment*. Off her bookshelf.

She woke the next morning and knew it was Sunday. Twenty-six years later, it still amazed him. He often boasted about it. He didn't sleep much himself, but he'd married a woman who did. He loved that. It had always been good. He still looked at her while she slept. She was still beautiful.

He'd been a different kind of eejit back then. He never went to restaurants, because they were bourgeois. He remembered actually saying that. There was Bewley's on Westmoreland Street, where you could get a fry or shepherd's pie – the people's food. Where you queued up and carried your own tray. Where they didn't throw out the junkies. That was the only place he'd go to. Not that he'd wanted to eat with the junkies. He kept well away from them. But he liked the fact that they could go into Bewley's, sit down and stay as long as they wanted. There was room for them. And the old women with their cakes and pots of tea, and journalists from the *Irish Times* across the street, and people who'd missed their bus and came in to get out of the rain. The famous Bewley's coffee was dreadful, but he only found that out later, when real coffee came to Dublin. And even if he'd known, it wouldn't have mattered. Good coffee would have been bourgeois. Along with suits and new cars and flats with more than two rooms and classical music and all the other things he couldn't cope with.

Then she phoned him one night. The strange man from the flat beside the payphone in the hall shouted up the stairs. Tom went down and picked up the phone.

—Hi.

It was her.

—Hi.

It was Tuesday. Nine o'clock. He'd been watching the News.

—I'm still in town, she said. —Working late. Will we go for something to eat?

And he'd said Yes. He was twenty minutes from her and he ran part of the way. He met her outside the Lebanese restaurant he'd walked past every day for years. They went in, and down the wooden steps to the basement. They ate in the damp, and he loved it. Not the food. Food never grabbed him. Not then or since. He liked it, but it was good or great – that was it. It was never delicious or sublime. He was a writer, but he'd never written about food. There wasn't a banana or a biscuit in anything he'd done.

It was her eating the food and talking about it – that was what he'd loved. Stuffing her mouth, laughing. A fat belly dancer came out of the Ladies with a tape recorder and an anorak. She plugged it in, hit the button, climbed out of the anorak, and danced in the couple of inches that were left between the tables. She knocked over the salt on theirs. They were the only customers. He couldn't wait to clap.

They went back to his place, because he needed his bag for work in the morning. They lay on his bed, pushed against each other because of the dead springs beneath them, and listened to the drunk in the next room trying to open a tin of stew or dog food.

—You don't have to live here, she said, quietly.

—It's fine.

—It isn't, she said.—It's fucking awful. Move in with me.

She slept and he looked at her. He slept for a while. She was still asleep when he had to leave for work. He sat on the chair beside the bed. He missed his bus.

He was a teacher then. He'd loved college, UCD, from the first day, and decided he'd stay. He saw himself lecturing on the contemporary novel to a room full of twenty-year-old women. He'd ended up teaching seven-year-old boys how to button their coats and say their prayers in Irish. But he liked it. For five years. Great kids – wild kids. With wild parents. Some of the mothers had frightened him. Tough, sexy birds in shiny track-suits. A bit desperate and mad; the sexy days were numbered and they knew it. He'd gone for a drink after work once, with a few of the other staff. He was at the bar, waiting for his pint – and one of the mothers was right beside him.

—Happy Christmas, sir, she said.

And she kissed him – on the 23rd of October. She grabbed his jacket and her tongue went into his mouth.

He tasted Coke and cheese 'n' onion. She took her mouth away, but she held on to his jacket.

—There, she said.

She smiled.

Her husband had come with her to the last parent–teacher meeting. He'd given Tom permission to use corporal punishment on their son.

—You can batter the little cunt, he'd said.—Any time.

An angry unemployed man who'd have been just as angry if he'd had a job.

But Tom, in the pub, didn't panic. He didn't look around for the husband. He didn't pull his jacket from her grip. If she'd asked him did he want to go outside and ride her against the back wall, behind the crates of empties, he'd have gone with her. It was politics, saying yes to a working-class woman with an unemployed husband. But she didn't ask. She let go of his jacket and went back to her friends, more blonde mothers in tracksuits who cheered as she got nearer to them. It was then he'd decided to get out of teaching.

But he'd liked it. And he'd believed in it. Teaching the little sons of men and women who'd never known work. Giving them that bit of power. And teaching was how he'd met Tara. He didn't remember much about the job but writing about it had given him his route out. He wrote a weekly column for a magazine called *Holy Dublin*. He'd started as a kind of Marxist man-about-town, but he'd run out of things to write about, because Dublin was such a dreary kip and he hardly ever went out. So he began to write about teaching. Most of it was lies – he didn't use his own name: *Notes from the Chalkface*, by Paddy Orwell. He even made himself a secondary teacher, teaching much older kids in a co-ed school. He met Tara one day when he brought in his copy.

He heard her before he saw her.

—Where's the fucking stapler?

That 'g'. He opened the reception door. She was searching the desk drawer with a cheerful violence that he thought was lovely. She looked at him. Big eyes, mouth, small ears, the hair.

—Hello, she said.

—Hi, he said.—I have my – my column here.

—Oh, great. Which one are you?

—*Notes from the Chalkface.*

—I love that fucking thing, she said.—It's a fucking hoot.

He took the pages from his school bag.

—Paddy Orwell, she said.

—It's not my real name.

—I love that, she said. —That's so fucking cool.

—Thanks.

—I'm new, she said.

He gave up teaching a month later. He told her about the mother kissing him in the pub – she loved it. It was a weird thing to be doing in Ireland in the eighties, giving up a job. But the guilt was alleviated by the fact that he no longer had a job to give up. He was half unemployed, one of the people. And he could stay in bed with Tara. It was probably the last exciting, unpredictable thing he ever did.

Now, more than twenty-five years later, he was sitting in bed, watching her sleep. His back hurt, he was frightened, but she was exactly the same. She was a grandmother, but the same. She'd slept through the recession, the boom, and she was sleeping through the new recession. She'd slept through the anxieties, terrors, poisonings, the joys and shite of marriage and children. He had cancer of the colon – he'd found out that afternoon, and he hadn't told her yet – but for now he didn't care. He had the cancer, she didn't – and that felt like success. It wasn't sentimentality. It was a physical thing, like a soft hand on the back of his neck.

He wouldn't die – he wasn't going to die. There was a good chance he wouldn't die – the specialist had said.

There was once, their eldest child stopped breathing. He came downstairs, out of bed, and sat between them on the couch. They argued over Aaron's head about who was going to bring him back upstairs. They were both a bit pissed – they were on three or four bottles of wine a night back then.

—I did it last time.

—You didn't. You weren't even here the last time.

Nothing too angry or meant. But they didn't notice that the child was dying until she gave up on the row and went to pick him up. Then they were suddenly sober and brilliant. He ran to the kitchen and rang for an ambulance. She managed to get some breath into Aaron, by massaging his chest or something, and she was putting on his coat – he was even helping her, lifting his arms. There was no sign of the ambulance, so Tom rang for a taxi. He told them it was an emergency, and there was one outside the front gate in thirty seconds – it seemed that quick. He ran out with Aaron in his arms, bouncing on his shoulder. The house wasn't far from the children's hospital on Temple Street, so he was there in five minutes, getting out of the taxi, trying to make sure Aaron's head didn't whack the door. The taxi driver wouldn't take money. The hospital would, though. They wanted a tenner before they'd let him into the A&E. He remembered switching Aaron to his other shoulder so he could get at his wallet. He even remembered giving the woman behind the hatch two fivers and watching her write the receipt. Aaron was watching her too, wheezing but okay.

—Good lad, good lad.

It was asthma. A nurse saw that before a doctor had looked at him. She put him up on a bed and got him to sit back against the pillow, and started to put some sort of plastic mask over his nose and mouth.

—Look at this yoke, Aaron, she said.—Will you put it on yourself or will I do it?

—What is it? Tom asked.

—A nebuliser, she said.—It'll open the poor lungs for him. It's just a spray, really, with the medicine in it. The easiest way to get it into them. And they love the drama.

She smiled, and he smiled. He saw how it worked now, the clear plastic pipe running from a box in the wall to the mask. Aaron didn't object as she put it over his face.

—Good lad, Tom said.—You're great.

He found a spare chair and sat beside Aaron. The

place was packed. There wasn't an empty bed, and some of the children were lying across two or three chairs, depending on the length of the child. Most of them had nebulisers. All the hissing and wheezing, the white-blue skin, the strange calm – it was terrifying, and lovely. The courage of his own lad, and the other children. A broken leg or a burn victim would have ruined it. He was there for three hours, more.

Later, he sat on the steps outside the hospital with Aaron, waiting for a taxi. Four in the morning. Aaron was wide awake, deep inside his coat. It was freezing, and absolutely windless. Tom could feel the dirt in the fog. There were men, four of them, standing at the corner of Hardwicke Street. They had a fire going in a barrel – a brazier. They stood around it, in jackets that looked much too thin.

—Why have they a fire? Aaron asked.

His breathing was grand, not a bother on him.

—They're cold, Tom said.

—Why don't they go to their houses?

—They want to stop other men from selling drugs, Tom said. —It's why they're out so late. Concerned Parents, they're called. It's sad.

They said nothing else. They watched the men and the fire in the barrel and waited for the taxi.

She was awake when they got home. Lying in bed, well under the duvet. She lifted it, so Aaron could get in beside her.

—Asthma, Tom said.

She smiled, and kissed Aaron's forehead.

Tom got into the bed. He leaned across Aaron, touched the top of her head. She smiled. She closed her eyes. She opened them, and closed them again. He lay there. She was asleep again. He listened to her, and to Aaron. He'd get a book tomorrow. He'd read it – they'd read it – and know enough about asthma, quickly. About broncho-spasm and allergens. About the inhalers and dust mites and mattress and pillow covers. They'd get rid of the carpets and the curtains, get blinds instead, and polish the floorboards. They'd sign petitions and phone the local politicians to make Dublin a smokeless zone. Aaron would be fine. He'd get into fights, he'd play his foot-ball. He'd go drinking in St Anne's Park, in the pissing rain, with his inhaler in his pocket. He'd join a band, he'd smoke, he'd stroll up Kilimanjaro. He'd come home one morning and tell them they were going to be grand-parents, and make them both shockingly happy.

Tom sat up a bit straighter now, in the bed. He looked at her, sleeping.

ACKNOWLEDGEMENTS

The author would like to thank Deborah Treisman, Cressida Leyshon, Nick Hornby, Joseph O'Connor, Neil Gaiman, Al Sarrantonio, Dan Franklin, Paul Slovak, Charlotte Northedge, Oona Frawley and the late David Marcus.

RODDY DOYLE was born in Dublin in 1958. He is the author of eight novels, two collections of stories, and *Rory & Ita*, a memoir of his parents. He won the Booker Prize in 1993 for *Paddy Clarke Ha Ha Ha*. He lives and works in Dublin.